THE BLOOMING OF ALISON BRENNAN

KATH ENGEBRETSON

Published 2021 by Next Chapter

Edited by Manuscript Appraisal Agency

Cover art by CoverMint

For Samuel, Reilly, Samara, Rishi, Jesse, Eyla and Lana

CHAPTER 1

STELLA GOODALL

TUESDAY, 2 FEBRUARY

SHE STEPPED INTO MY OFFICE AND LOOKED AROUND.

Later I would learn that this was a habit of hers. She took in the details of spaces.

Today was the first day back at school after the summer holidays, and already the sun beat with a headachy glare against the window. I'd drawn the blind, and warmed some drops of sandalwood oil in a burner. The irises I'd bought on the way to work stood stiffly in a vase on my desk. Their pointy sapphire buds would open by the afternoon.

The office was in the original sandstone building at the front of the school, and its north-facing window framed hectares of green playing fields.

In my first week here, I had consigned the dingy school-issue brown chairs and stained yellow rug to a remote store-room. At the Salvos in Glenferrie Road I found two heavy, seventies style armchairs. They were wide and solid, big enough to curl your legs up, and to support your back and neck. Joe, the caretaker, collected them in his van and wrestled them inside, dabbing at his sweaty face with a big handker-chief. They were now covered in a soft, sky-blue fabric.

From home I brought the faded circular mat from my

study. It was thinning in places but it had a lovely traditional design of interlinked flower-like splotches of rich cobalt and mauve. At the same Salvos store I found a kitschy, fake-marble, art-deco coffee table in a wavy rectangular shape. Its blue-grey undertones picked up the blue of the chairs. Against the back wall was my desk, again standard issue, and it held my computer, diary, a telephone and current files. It wasn't the main character in the room.

Under the window there was a low fridge where I kept cold water, and on top was a jug and some mugs for tea and coffee. There was one framed print — a 1950s watercolour of the curve of the Yarra, east of Princes Bridge, looking towards the city. Just the one print. The boys and girls I saw in this room didn't need to endure happy snaps of my family.

Alison Brennan.

I knew from her file that she was sixteen. She was of medium height, slim and athletic. Her long, glossy, brown hair was tied back with the regulation red and white ribbons. She was very pale, obviously nervous. The paleness emphasised the unusual blue, almost navy, of her eyes. Her school dress was freshly pressed, and she wore her white socks and school shoes with the easy grace of someone who didn't know she was beautiful.

'Good morning, Alison. Please sit down.'

I brought two glasses of water to the table and pushed one towards her. I noticed her looking at details — the straight, neat irises, the print, the colourful rug. She took the water in both hands but didn't drink. I wondered if she regretted making the appointment.

'So, Alison, Year Eleven?'

She nodded.

I knew from her file that she was a good student, a good all-rounder really. Her main strengths were in the humanities, but she kept up in Maths and Science. She was in the middle school girls' swimming team. There were no prefect or SRC positions listed on her file, but she had never been in trouble — no suspensions, disciplinary meetings or concerned letters to her parents.

Her school fees were paid by her grandfather, Judge Colin Brennan. I knew him by sight from his attendance at the annual Parent Information evenings, at which I was obliged to speak, and I recalled that he was rather formidable.

That was all. In her four years at the school, Alison had never drawn attention to herself.

It was difficult to get past her nervousness. She held the glass of water close, like a shield.

'How can I help you, Alison?' I sipped my water and waited until the silence became too heavy. 'You have two big years ahead. Are you worried about the workload?' It was a common concern at this time of the year.

'Yes,' she said, very softly.

'What worries you about it? You've always done well at school, haven't you?'

'Yes, but it's more important now. I have to get a good ATAR score. I have to get into uni.'

Her vehemence was surprising. At the beginning of Year Eleven, most students didn't talk about getting into university as if their entire life depended on it. The options were still fluid.

'But that's possible; your marks have always been good.'

More silence, then again, ever so softly, she practically whispered, 'I can't study at home.'

She looked ashamed, as if she had blurted out something sacrilegious. Her face was red. She stood up suddenly and walked towards the print on the wall, standing with her back to me, examining it.

'It's lovely, isn't it?' I remarked.

'Yes, it's restful. It looks as if it was a hot day, something like today.'

'Melbourne before Southbank and the Casino.' I sounded inane, even to myself. I waited for her to sit down again.

'Why can't you study at home? Is it too noisy? Too crowded?'

'It's crowded all right,' she muttered. She stared at the floor.

Again I waited. I knew that she had no brothers or sisters.

Finally she looked up, looked at me directly. She seemed to have decided that she would let me help, but I could see that she had to dredge it out of herself. She'd take my help for now, but if I wasn't careful she'd close down.

'You see, Mrs Goodall ... um, well ... it's my parents.'

Again she blushed. Was it shame, embarrassment, or something else?

'They're not like other people.'

'Oh?' I queried, puzzled and eager to learn in what way.

She took a deep breath. 'Our house is very dirty. More than dirty, it's filthy. There are fleas, cockroaches and rats. My parents never throw anything away and they never clean. There's rubbish piled up everywhere, in some places to the ceiling. There's nowhere to sit, no table to eat at. Everything is covered high with junk. Even my room. They even use my room to store their junk. I have to climb over it to get to my bed.'

She began to cry then, big sobs, as if her resentment, confusion and anger had burst a dam.

I put a box of tissues on the table close to her. 'They're hoarders?' I asked.

'Yes, I've read about it. It's a mental illness. Not that Mum and Dad understand that. They're embarrassed about it, but they don't seem to be able to help themselves. It's disgusting, and ... dangerous.'

'How long has it been like this?'

'All of my life, but I hide it. I never have friends at home. I'm too embarrassed. The neighbours talk about us.

You can't see the house for the weeds and junk in the front yard.'

She'd stopped crying now, but her eyes were red and swollen.

I could imagine how hard this was for her. At sixteen, girls were constantly in and out of each other's homes, sleeping overnight, making snacks in the kitchen, studying, calling friends, watching TV and movies, giggling in front of social media.

'We can't cook in the kitchen because there are cockroaches in the oven, and the stovetop is used as another shelf for junk. I know there's rotting food in the fridge because I can smell it, but I can't bear to open it. The hot water service broke down two years ago and my parents are too embarrassed to get someone into fix it, so we don't have hot water. The bath is full of rubbish like everywhere else, and the shower is blocked. When you flush the toilet it floods on to the junk on the floor. Everything smells. The washing machine is full of mould.'

I had to conceal my horror. I didn't want to scare her off. 'How do you eat and keep clean?'

'I work out at the gym most mornings, and I have a shower there. I get a coffee and toast at the gym, and then I come to school. I buy lunch at school, and for dinner we get takeaway. The litter just gets added to the pile. We haven't put the bins out for over a year. So yeah, there's so many rats?' She was crying again. 'I've even been bitten by rats, and every day I have new fleabites. They're in the beds and in all the rubbish.'

'How do you keep your clothes clean?' I asked. She was immaculate.

'Once a week I take all my washing to the laundromat. I dry it and press it there. There's one cupboard up high in my room where I can keep my clothes. It's the only one in the house that's not full of rubbish.'

'Sheets? Towels?'

'I wash my own once a week.'

'Sorry for all the questions. It helps if I have some details. You don't have to tell me anything you don't want to.'

'It's okay.'

'How did you manage when you were younger? When you couldn't go to the laundromat or the gym by yourself?'

'I didn't manage. But I thought it was normal. I never went to other houses. It wasn't until Grade Six that I began to realise how different our house was from other peoples'. I must have smelled. I had fleas in my hair.' She touched her shiny hair, remembering. 'I had a friend that year, a Vietnamese girl. I went to her house a lot, and I picked up things from her — how to wash my hair, to have a shower every day, how to keep my clothes clean. She never judged me, and never asked questions. Her name was Lo-an. Then she went to a different high school and we lost touch.'

I didn't know what to say. Now I was the one to stand, to walk about, and look through a chink in the blind to brilliant red and white geraniums in beds along the path that led to the playing fields.

What an effort she has to make, I thought, *to come to school clean and fresh, her hair brushed, her clothes pressed, her socks white and her shoes shiny. She has to keep up the charade of a normal life with her classmates and teachers, and now she has the VCE workload to contend with.*

With my back to her, I indulged for a second a wild fury with her parents. But my feelings were not the point. I had to help her to find ways to cope in that horrible environment.

'See what I mean about getting a good ATAR? If I can get into a uni in the country, maybe Gippsland, Bendigo, even Wollongong or Armidale in New South Wales, I can move away and live in student accommodation.'

I sat down again, and faced her. I resisted taking her hands. It was not my job to be motherly.

'Don't get the wrong impression, Mrs Goodall. You know, they're great parents in lots of other ways. They're kind, and they're very proud of me. I know they love me. They just don't cope with life. I don't know why.' She hesitated, and then challenged me, clear-eyed. 'You won't tell anyone, will you?'

'Of course not. We'll work on this together, Alison.'

CHAPTER 2

ALISON BRENNAN

TUESDAY, 2 FEBRUARY

I DIDN'T TELL HER EVEN HALF OF IT.

I didn't tell her about Grandpa, about how I hadn't seen him for four years because of the fight he had with Mum last time he came to our house. It was at the end of Grade Six. It was a Saturday, and he turned up without telling them. When he saw the house, he went crazy.

He yelled at Mum. 'What's wrong with you, Bernadette? How can you live like this? What about Alison's safety?'

That was the first time I realised that our house was dangerous, as well as dirty and smelly.

'One dropped match and it could all go up,' Grandpa bellowed.

I thought about running away to hide in the high weeds in the backyard, but it was like I was nailed to the floor. Grandpa was very tall and scary.

Mum just stood there, twisting her hands, fiddling with her hair. You could tell she was terrified.

Grandpa seemed really puzzled. 'I don't understand it, Bernadette,' he said more softly. It was like he was talking to a naughty child caught playing in the mud. 'I can see how it might happen with that useless blighter you live with, but you weren't brought up like this.'

I didn't understand it then. All I knew was that Mum and Dad would never let anyone into the house.

But I now knew that they needed help, not yelling. They didn't know how to be any other way.

I didn't know how, but Grandpa had found out that Mum and Dad hadn't enrolled me in a secondary school. That was why he came over. It wouldn't have occurred to them that they had to make calls, visit the schools in the area, and make a choice. All the other kids had been talking for months about where they'd go. The parents talked about it all the time too, standing at the school gate, competing with each other.

'Oh, Melanie's going to Mc Robb, you know. Yes, she's so bright; they offered her a place right away.'

Or 'Christopher is going to Scotch of course; all the boys in the family go there.'

But Mum and Dad never saw any other parents. It was just the three of us, a little human triangle, hidden away in our dirty house.

Grandpa went ballistic when he found out that I wasn't enrolled anywhere. 'I'll have to find her a school, I suppose. It's far too late for any of the decent Catholic girls schools. We'll have to take what we can get now.'

That's how I ended up at this big co-ed college on St Kilda Road. Grandpa knew the Principal. Apparently he was the son of one of the judges Grandpa worked with before he retired.

Anyway, that particular day he took Mum and me to a motel. I didn't know where Dad was; he disappeared when Grandpa started yelling. Grandpa got cleaners into the house to shovel out the rubbish. He sent a plumber to fix the blocked shower and kitchen sink, and a handyman to put the cupboard doors back on. He got a gardening company to throw out the rubbish in the front and back yards and to cut down the weeds.

On the Monday he enrolled me in school and took me to get my uniform, books and stationery. He hardly said anything during all of this. His face looked really angry, but when he dropped me at home he kissed me and told me to ring him about anything, any time that I wanted. Then he went away without saying goodbye to Mum and Dad, and we hadn't seen him since.

That was four years ago.

It was good in the house for a month or two, then the rubbish started to pile up again.

DURING MY MEETING with Mrs Goodall, she asked me to write a list of places I could go to, to study. And she said that she was going to arrange for me to use the school library at weekends.

Writing the list made me think of Grandpa. He told me I could phone him, but I never had. It would seem like I was taking sides with him against Mum and Dad. But I kept remembering the house at Golden Beach. It was his holiday house, although he lived there now since he retired. I used to go there a lot when I was in primary school. He'd pick me up in his big car and we'd always get hamburgers along the way.

The house was like a huge box on stilts. You climbed steep steps at the back, and when you walked in all you could see was ocean. Grandpa never drew curtains or blinds. The light or the dark just came right in. I used to love standing at the big front window watching the waves march in like soldiers in a battle, and then falling over as if it was all a big joke. Grandpa told me that if I was a bird and flew directly across that ocean I would come to Tasmania. Sometimes at home I would imagine that I was that bird, and that I could fly for days over the ocean to land in a new place, clean and green and sunny.

I hadn't been to Grandpa's house since he had that fight with Mum.

Mrs Goodall wanted us to meet once a week. She said we would work out some 'strategies' and make sure that there were 'appropriate' places for me to study. She used all this counsellor-type language.

She also asked me to talk to Mum and Dad about respecting my 'private space' in my bedroom. She said that I would have to be firm with them, but I had a right to have a tidy, neat place where I could study.

She wanted me to tell Mum and Dad that they couldn't put any more of their stuff in my room, and to ask them for help in moving out the rubbish that was already there. She asked me if I felt comfortable talking to Mum and Dad about it, and I said not really, but I'd do it. I was going to do it before I met her next time.

At the end of our meeting, she asked me how I felt. I could feel that my eyes were puffy from crying, but what I liked about her was that she wasn't all clammy and motherly, putting her arms around you, and getting too close. She just pushed the box of tissues towards me and listened. That was the best thing — she listened.

How did I feel about telling her?

I said that I was relieved, and that was true, but I didn't tell her that something inside me was shrivelling up in horror, now that I had told her our family's worst, deepest secret.

CHAPTER 3

LEO BRENNAN

TUESDAY, 2 FEBRUARY

THE OLD MAN'S A BULLY.

He terrorised Bernadette, made it obvious that she wasn't the daughter he'd hoped for. She was always withdrawn; she hid behind our mum. But it was the year I was at Melbourne University, when I was nineteen and she was twenty-one, that the agoraphobia took over.

She went out less and less, and eventually refused to go anywhere unless Mum went with her. She hid in her room, in that big, cold house. She read, wrote in her diary, watched soap operas on television, shuffled around doing chores, and collected junk. She seemed to have decided that that was going to be her life, and for years she clung to Mum as a stranded sailor might cling to an upturned boat. Then Mum died and Harry rescued her, or so it must have seemed to Bernie.

By fourteen years of age, I knew that I was gay, but nothing coerced me to reveal that to 'the Judge' — our dad. It was strange that I couldn't admit such a basic fact about myself, but back then it was still a stigma, and in a Catholic family like mine, it was considered a serious sin. It would have been hard for anyone who didn't grow up in that house to understand how deeply Catholic it was. Even my name, Leo, came from the Judge's favourite Pope, Leo XIII, champion of workers' rights and unions, but also defender of the right to private property and free enterprise. Old Leo was the Judge's hero.

I couldn't talk about being gay at school either. It was a bastion of Catholic conservatism, and the priests and other boys had names for boys like me. So I played football and cricket, and I laughed at fag jokes. Sometimes at lunchtime, I escaped into the art studio and took down the heavy books of paintings from their high shelf. I pored over the colours and shapes, lost myself in the harsh landscapes, the gentle watercolours, the dreamlike impressionists. I was mesmerised by the greens, greys and blues of outback Australia, and the swirling shapes and colours of the abstracts. Recalling those magical paintings helped me to sleep at night.

Art was considered fine until the end of Year Ten, when the Judge decreed that I was to study serious subjects that would help me to get into Law. It was an article of faith that I would follow him into Melbourne University, and not go to one of those modern, 'lefty newcomers' that he scorned. I wanted to be a good son. Bernie had disappointed him, so he focused his authority on me. I let him; indeed I craved his approval. The smallest nod of his head in recognition of some achievement could keep me going for days.

I separated myself from Mum. I couldn't admit how much I wanted and needed her. She brought hot chocolate to my room every night and always hesitated to leave, wanting to talk, but I brushed her off.

'Everything alright, darling?'

'Yes, Mum, everything's fine.'

Then she'd kiss me. She'd tell me that she loved me, and despite the wall I'd built between us, I waited nightly for her declaration.

So I excelled academically, captained the senior football

team in my final year, pretended I was interested in girls, and late at night drifted to sleep to dreams of soft-limbed boys from school.

I went to Melbourne University, intent on taking a path through the city's best law firms, and securing a seat on the bench, replicating my father's life. I was too caught up in it all to see that it couldn't last.

One day, stepping into the shower, preparing to put on my armour for another day, I was hit by a tidal wave of darkness and futility. My defences crumbled in an instant. I couldn't turn on the tap, couldn't do anything except fall against the wall and slide to the floor.

I curled into a foetal position, reduced to helplessness. I sobbed quietly at first, and then I lost my cultivated control. The sobbing became a howl, and the howl became a scream. I banged my head on the floor, didn't care what happened, how much noise I made. I didn't know if I was there for hours or minutes. All I knew was that I was looking into a fathomless darkness that I couldn't escape. In a perverse way, I wanted it to reach up its slimy tentacles and suck me in.

I was in hell.

The cleaner found me. She was a Filipina, much coveted for her skills by the matrons of Toorak, and given to expletive-laden scorn at their condescension. She covered my nakedness, cradled my head on her lap, and rocked me with lullaby words.

Summoned from one of her committees, Mum called an ambulance, and a Crisis Assessment Team took me to the Melbourne Clinic. I spent five months there, numb among other sedated shadows. I was cared for by a white-haired psychiatrist, a death camp tattoo just visible on his forearm. With infinite compassion he took my psyche apart, as one might disassemble a child's toy, and put it back into something recognisable and authentic.

The Judge visited me periodically in the clinic, but always had to leave quickly; he was very uncomfortable while there. Mum came often. We would sit in the sun, or in the corner of the library, not always talking. Towards the end, when I was almost ready to leave, we would go to Victoria Street for a bowl of noodles.

That was when we found each other again.

One day, over a pot of tea in a tiny Vietnamese restaurant, I finally told her that I was gay. I watched her eyes. No change.

She picked up my hand from the plastic tablecloth and kissed it. That was all. She knew and she didn't care.

The Judge offered me money to convalesce in Europe. He thought that once I was over my foolish breakdown, I would resume my destined path — as if I could pick it up like a suitcase I had put down for an hour or so. But there was no going back. I took a quarter of the money he offered and lost myself in India, another displaced white man in cheap drawstring pants, ragged T-shirt and dirty sandals.

I merged into India's scurrying, surging masses. I lived in hovels, or in a corner of someone's room, and I ate rice and dhal from street stalls. When Mum sent money for my birthday, I bought my first real camera, strapping it to my body when I slept and when I pushed through the streaming crowds. The camera was my passport to a longed for life of the imagination.

From Mumbai, I travelled north by train and photographed sari-clad women emerging with radiant faces from the sacred waters of the Ganges. During the mad exuberance of the Holi festival, I filled my viewfinder with images of joyous Hindus covered in multi-coloured powders. At the Golden Temple Pond in Amritsar, my camera captured the moment that the morning sun turned the holy waters bronze, as a turbaned Sikh bathed lost in meditation. As my guru and guide, I adopted Krishna the god of youth, music, courage and love and had his child-like image tattooed on my chest.

I learnt to take photographs by watching and waiting — waiting for the exact play of light on water, for the very moment a smile broke across a child's face, for the instant the setting sun dropped behind a mountain. In a mosque in Mumbai at the end of Ramadan, I photographed rows of Muslim men bent over in prayer. Their straight lines of reverence, their discipline, and their indifference to distractions, filled me with wonder. I had never experienced such enthrallment with the entity I had been taught to call God.

With each photograph my happiness grew, and little by little I became visible to myself again.

Eventually, I was ready to go home. I wanted to see Mum and to tell my story, my real story, to the Judge. I didn't return to the Toorak mansion, but lived in a shabbily comfortable share house in Camberwell while I found my life. I began my photography business tentatively, doing favours for relatives of friends, taking snaps of chocolate-stained little faces at children's birthday parties. Whenever I could, I roamed city streets with my camera, documenting graffiti before it disappeared, trying to expose the beauty of grungy lanes and the juxtaposition of skyscrapers with bluestone cobbles. I would go to the beach or into the bush to practise with my camera, mastering the art of watching and waiting.

When one of my photos — red and gold autumn leaves in the Dandenong hills — won a prize at a local gallery, I began to call myself a photographer.

TRENT and I fell in love by accident. He was the bulky, bearded best man at a friend's wedding and I was the fidgety photographer, bothering everyone for a spontaneous shot. We thought we were as different as two people could be, but long after the bridal pair had left to a round of tipsy cheers, we talked, as waiters cleared around us.

Our love was a comfortable, ordinary thing. We rode our bikes by the Yarra, hiked in the country, me lugging my camera, argued about football, and ate at small, local restaurants. We knitted out lives together like two sleeves of one of those thick, warm jumpers you threw on against the Melbourne nights.

When we knew that we wanted to be together forever, and we moved into our rented cottage in Port Melbourne, the cottage we eventually bought, I knew it was time to put some organisation into my business. My website said it all.

LB Photography: Every imaginable celebration: weddings, divorces, christenings, birthdays, bar and bat mitzvahs, anniversaries, graduations; I cover them all, anywhere, at any time. I will help you to make your occasion joyous and memorable.

At the Esplanade market on St Kilda's foreshore, I sold my other photographs, those I took in the bush, or in the city streets, or trudging across sand dunes to the beach. I was always sending my photos to outback and travel magazines, hoping for a commission that would take me away into the Australian landscape, where my camera could record its colours and moods, and where I could again feel the freedom I felt in India.

I knew I was like the Judge. I was tall like him, and I had the thick, blond hair that he had when he was younger. I talked like him, with the same vocal timbre and inflections, and used the same kind of vocabulary. But I hoped I was kinder and less hasty to judge others, just as Mum was.

I rang the Judge every Sunday to check on him. I was

going to insist on my existence. I visited Bernie, dragged myself into that stinking house and tried to make her talk to me.

It was me who told the Judge that they hadn't enrolled Alison in a secondary school. Someone had to. Bernie wouldn't leave the house, and poor dull Harry didn't know what to do.

I thought about Alison all the time; I adored her. Whenever I could, I extricated her from that frightful house and brought her here for one of Trent's pastas or roasts. We talked about everything — except her parents. She was intensely loyal.

IT WAS PROBABLY time that we drove down to see the Judge, although he was rude to Trent last time we went. He mellowed when he saw the bottle of merlot Trent had brought. The old hypocrite! Chester dug up one of his tomato plants.

'Get that bloody dog out of my garden,' he bellowed.

Chester was a Jack Russell. They had to dig — it was a moral obligation.

So we planned to go there at Easter, even knowing that the Judge wouldn't be happy to see us.

CHAPTER 4

ROD WILDING

WEDNESDAY, 10 FEBRUARY

I THOUGHT I'D SEEN EVERYTHING.

I had worked for local councils in Melbourne for twenty years, but I only started with the Yarra Council a few months ago, so I didn't know the house. This summer was a scorcher — one of the hottest on record for the state — so we were doing spot checks for fire risk areas, overgrown yards, rubbish lying around. The last thing we wanted was a fire in this densely populated suburb.

The call came from a neighbour who said he'd made complaints about this particular dwelling before. He was especially worried now, he said, because he'd seen one of the inhabitants smoking and discarding butts in long, dry grass in front of the house.

So I went there with the council literature on fire prevention and safety. If necessary, we'd get machinery in to slash the long grass and trim tree branches away from the electrical cables.

But this house was one out of the box.

Overgrown trees obscured the windows of the house. A wooden picket fence had fallen in on itself, so you had to scramble over it, and the tinder dry weeds in front of the house were waist-high in places. Fire would rip through it.

I made my way to the front door through piles of rubbish. Broken bicycles, an old TV, furniture blasted by heat and rain, the body of a rusted car stripped of its parts, an upended child's swing, piles of smelly household rubbish buzzing with flies.

I felt sick at what I might find, even though I'd been through this kind of thing before. I was a believing man, and at times like these my impulse was to send out a prayer. 'Please God, don't let there be kids here.'

The door wasn't locked because the handle had come off, but something behind the door prevented me from pushing it inwards. I knocked. No response. I knocked again. Then there was a shuffling behind the door, a sliding, falling noise, like things being pushed out of the way. I then heard a female voice.

'Who is it? We're not interested in what you're selling.'

'I'm not selling anything, Ma'am. It's Rod Wilding from the Yarra Council. I'm here to advise you on fire prevention. If you'll open the door I can show you my ID.'

'No, go away, we're alright with fire prevention.'

'Well, no Ma'am, I'm afraid you're not. Your front yard is a fire hazard. You'll need to clear it right away. If you'll open the door and talk to me, I can show you what needs to be done.'

'Go away.'

'Is anyone else in the house with you, Ma'am?'

I heard a male voice say, 'What's going on?' And then the door was dragged halfway open. He was tall, broad and unsmiling. Suspicious.

The woman hid behind him. I got the impression of someone short and plump, and despite the heat, she was wearing a long-sleeved cardigan. The smell from the house rushed at me. It was a mixture of rotting food, mould, all kinds of thing I couldn't name.

I held up my ID. 'Rod Wilding from the council.'

'What do you want?'

'You're going to need to clear around your house, Sir. This is the worst fire season in years. We're encouraging all residents to do everything they can to reduce risk. Here are some council pamphlets that will inform you about the fire safety by-laws.'

He made no move to take them, but stepped across to shield the inside of the house from view. Before he did I caught a glimpse of high piles of paper and litter, and similar jumbles of rubbish as in the front yard.

He wanted to get rid of me.

'Yeah, mate, I know it needs doing. Been putting it off. I'll get on to it. Thanks for the reminder. By the end of the week, it will be done.'

I didn't believe him, but I'd done what I had to do. 'How many people live here, Sir?'

'Only me and the missus.'

'Good. I'll give you a few days then come back.' I turned back towards the street and stumbled again over the broken fence. Just as I was about to start my car, someone else went in the way I'd come out, into that firetrap of a house.

It was a young girl in a school uniform — fifteen or sixteen years old.

As soon as I got back to the office I made a phone call to Child Protection Services. Someone had to check on that girl.

CHAPTER 5

ALISON BRENNAN

WEDNESDAY, 10 FEBRUARY

MUM WAS IN A STATE WHEN I GOT HOME FROM SCHOOL.

She was yelling at Dad, 'See what you've done. Because you won't cut the grass, now the council's after us.'

Dad grumbled back, 'I can't cut the grass because of all the stuff you've got out there that you won't let me throw away.'

'Don't talk to me,' she wailed. Then she cleared a patch on the couch and sat with her head in her hands. A pile of papers slid to the floor.

'He'll call Child Protection. They'll take Alison.'

I gradually got the story. A council guy had come to the house and told them it was a fire hazard. Of course it was, and on this hot day it was stifling. I could hardly breathe for the heat.

'Did you tell him I live here?' I asked.

'No,' Dad said. 'But he would have seen you. You came in as he left.'

This could go two ways, I thought. *He may decide not to get involved, or he may be conscientious and decide to report it.*

I didn't want Mum and Dad more upset, but after talking to Mrs Goodall, I was beginning to rebel. Something inside me, a small hope, wanted the man to be conscientious.

THEY CAME at seven o'clock in the evening, a man and a woman, about Uncle Leo's age, in their forties. Their names were Bruce and Marilyn. They had kind faces. At first, Mum wouldn't let them in. She thought she could talk to them through the door as she did with the council man, but they were persistent.

'It's only to discuss a complaint that came to our office. We won't keep you long, Bernadette,' Bruce said.

So they knew our names.

'What complaint?' Mum demanded, still refusing to open the door.

This wasn't going to work.

'It will be best if you handle this,' I said to Dad. I took Mum over to her seat on the couch and sat on its arm next to her.

At last Dad opened the door and they came through. I watched them carefully. They didn't register any shock at the state of the house; perhaps they'd seen this before. They didn't ask to sit down — it would have been pointless — but stood in a space that Dad cleared for them. The man spoke and the woman looked around.

Please don't go to the kitchen, don't ask about the hot water, don't badger Mum, she's fragile. The fears circled in my head.

But the woman, Marilyn, did go to the kitchen, picking her way through the rubble. The kitchen was the final horror. When she saw that she would know everything.

Dad began, apologetically, 'Sorry about the place. Things have got a bit beyond us.'

Bruce talked then about what they did, why they were there, and that they needed to make sure I was safe.

'She's safe,' Dad said.

Mum sat with her head down. Any minute she would try to disappear into her bedroom.

Finally Marilyn said, 'We need to speak to your daughter alone for a few moments, please.' She turned to me. 'Is there somewhere we can talk?'

I thought of the rest of the house, just as junked as this room. 'No. I'll come outside with you.'

So we stood on the overgrown nature strip and they asked me questions.

'How long has the house been like this?'

'All of my life.'

'The kitchen's unsafe. Where do you cook?'

'We don't.'

I decided not to make it anymore difficult for them. I told them everything that I'd told Mrs Goodall — about how I had learnt to look after myself, going to the gym to shower, buying food at the gym and at school, washing my things in the laundromat at the weekend. It was a relief to tell it to someone official.

The man was nice.

'It's serious, Alison,' he said. 'It's dangerous and unhealthy.'

'Please,' I answered, 'I cope okay. Don't make trouble for Mum. She's not well.'

'We're going to come back every week for a while to check on you,' he said. He gave me his card.

'Now, please be honest with us, do you need help?' Marilyn asked as she handed me her card too.

Yes, yes, yes, I need help — that little voice of hope whispered in my head.

But I took their cards, promised to call them if I needed to, and went inside to Mum and Dad.

Mum was still sitting on the couch, crying now. I was so used to making excuses for her that at first I didn't acknowledge the feeling that swelled inside me, like a balloon gradually inflating. It was fury… at Mum and her self-pity, and at Dad and his weakness. Fury at the situation they'd put me in, having to be monitored like an abused child.

'This isn't about you, Mum,' I said in a voice I'd never used with her before.

I then left the house, taking my phone. I knew what I had to do.

After four years, it was time.

CHAPTER 6

COLIN BRENNAN

THURSDAY, 11 FEBRUARY

I WENT TO THE BEACH EARLY, JUST AS IT WAS GETTING LIGHT.

The smudgy halo around the sun told me we were in for another scorcher. The CFA already had their board out announcing a total fire ban. A surfer was paddling, crouched over his board, and for an instant the rising sun outlined him in gold. Closer to the beach, the surf was dark and shadowy in that blue-grey shade it got before the full light. On the dunes, prickly whiskers of sea grass began to show.

I threw two lines out and secured them, then sat on my fold-up chair with my thermos of coffee. I wanted to think.

Alison had rung me last night. When I heard her voice after four years, my stomach turned over. She was a little girl when I last saw her, just about to leave primary school, and now she was sixteen. She sounded very grown up.

I was furious with Bernadette about the way they were making Alison live. *It's child abuse!* Oh the stench of that place. If they weren't my own family I'd go right to Human Services, but that would mean they'd take Alison away. Where would that leave her? With some dreadful foster family, probably.

Of course I could sue for custody, but Alison would hate that. Despite everything, she seemed to love her parents, and it was pitiful to see her trying to protect them. As it turned out, after I confronted Bernadette that day about the secondary schools, I cut ties with them. Perhaps it wasn't the best thing to do, because it meant I lost touch with Alison too. I told her to ring me any time she wanted, but until yesterday she hadn't. A child would always side with her parents.

I wasn't a talker, and I couldn't talk to my kids. During my years on the bench I saw too much cruelty and horror, stupidity and evil, too much derangement and violence. I kept it away, even from Mary, my wife, when she was alive. The parade of human misery I saw every day locked me up inside. I was afraid it gave me a magisterial air that I didn't always leave in the courtroom.

I wasn't a patient father. Bernadette was a mousy child, afraid of me, jumping at her own shadow. She clung to her mother, and whenever I tried to put some backbone into her, give her a push, she would crumble. Mary protected her.

Later, in her twenties, when she was incapacitated with anxiety, Mary took her to a psychiatrist, and she was diagnosed with anxiety-induced agoraphobia. At least there was a name for it. She was treated by the psychiatrist right up until Mary died, and then she fell apart completely.

With no one to be a shield between herself and the world, she made the house her prison, especially her room in which she stacked every kind of left-over she could find — books and clothes that had belonged to her mother, broken kitchen utensils, piles of paper, old toys, magazines, junk mail, things that should have been relegated to the rubbish bin. It was as if the rubbish was another wall of defence against the world. Then she found someone to take Mary's place, someone else she could hide behind.

Harry was the outside man we hired to keep the grounds tidy. He was a little simple, and older than Bernadette. After the cancer took Mary, he and Bernadette would talk in the garden. He must have persuaded Bernadette to go away with him, because she disappeared suddenly.

After a week or so, a letter informed me that they were living together, renting a flat in Fitzroy. I bought a house in Clifton Hill for her. What could I do, she had to have somewhere decent to live. I paid an allowance into her bank account every month. I thought Bernadette would have run away with anyone at that stage — no self-confidence and no judgment. That was eighteen or so years ago.

After Alison was born, they seemed to cope well enough. Harry was working then, at least intermittently, and while the house was messy, it was liveable. They would take Alison to kindergarten and then to school.

As Alison got older, though, Bernadette's agoraphobia got worse. She retreated into the house and let the filth build up. She became obese, never seemed to bathe. I would take Alison away during the school holidays and often I had to send cleaners in to scour the property and remove junk. After the last row, when I realised they hadn't enrolled Alison in a secondary school, I gave up. I shouldn't have done that. My stubbornness meant that I hadn't seen Alison for four years.

As for my son, Leo, the less said about him the better. Despite the fact that I paid a fortune to the Jesuits for twelve years, he had turned out to be a bloody wedding photographer. On Sundays, he sold his strange photos to the tourists on the Esplanade. He threw in a law degree at Melbourne University, and went slumming through India. Then he came back to tell me he was following his 'first love', photography, and moved into a dilapidated share house in Camberwell, after informing me that he was homosexual.

I can't abide that Trent fellow he lives with — a Homicide Detective no less. Dear God! You can't have homosexual cops, it shouldn't be allowed.

Leo rang me once a week, mainly to nag me about my blood pressure tablets and my alcohol intake.

As if it's any of his business — a nip or two of Scotch in the evenings and a little wine, that's all. I'm still strong and healthy, still walk for miles on the beach.

There's never been anyone for me except Mary. I wished I'd told her that more often. Mary would have known what to do about Alison. After she died, I stayed on the bench for a few more years, then sold the Toorak house and came down here to Golden Beach. I had the old shack demolished, and paid an architect to design this high, boxy two-storey house across the road from the beach.

It was a quiet village, just right for someone solitary like me. There was only a general store and a fish and chip shop, and golf and bowling clubs if you were inclined that way. I wasn't. You needed to go into Sale for supplies.

When she was small I'd bring Alison to Golden Beach for the school holidays. She loved the beach and she read or built sandcastles while I fished. Then we'd cook something together, usually fresh fish if they were biting. I never had to entertain her — she was a self-sufficient child.

I wasn't a success with Bernadette and Leo, too much 'the Judge'. But when Alison was small and we walked on the beach looking for unusual shells, she'd take my hand. Then I thought that maybe I could be a better grandfather than I was a father, that maybe there was a second chance.

I had no trouble occupying my time in my quiet retreat. The silence filled me like a living thing. I reached out for it, drew it in hungrily. The days went by quickly. I fished or walked on the beach. I was also writing my memoirs — wasn't everyone now? Even the most vapid 'celebrity' who once appeared on some deplorable reality show seemed to think they had something portentous to tell the world.

I tried some of the most notorious cases in Australian criminal history. I had sentenced paedophiles and rapists, child killers, murderers who had hacked their victims to pieces, gangland figures, crooked cops and politicians. They came from all walks of life, from the so-called 'leafy suburbs', to the most grimy housing commission areas. It was all going to come out in the book.

I wrote an occasional column on legal matters for *The Australian.* I was experimenting with native plants, to see what grew in this sandy soil. And once a month I drove to Melbourne to lunch with other retired judges, and I stayed over at 'the Club'. I read everything. This late in life I'd discovered the miraculous iPad, so I was no longer dependant on the limited regional library.

Anyway, now there was Alison.

When we spoke, we arranged for her to visit me for Easter and the school holidays. It was Ash Wednesday yesterday, so I went to the Cathedral in Sale to be reminded of my mortality, and I wore the ashy Cross on my forehead all day. I had given up wine for Lent, just the two shots of whisky in the evenings. Alison was to arrive on Good Friday afternoon, so I was going to miss the service this year, but we planned to go together to Easter Mass.

By nine that evening I was home, with a good-sized gummy shark, which I cleaned and filleted, steaming one fillet for breakfast with a thick slice of the bread I baked yesterday. I sat for a long time watching the ocean.

I must look for the Scrabble set today. Alison and I might play in the evenings.

CHAPTER 7
ALISON BRENNAN
SATURDAY, 20 FEBRUARY

IT TOOK ME MORE THAN TWO WEEKS TO WORK UP TO IT, BUT yesterday I did what Mrs Goodall said I should.

When I came home from school, they were sitting on the couch, close together, on the only space that wasn't covered with stuff. They were watching *The Bold and the Beautiful*. I climbed over the rubbish and found the remote, and then I turned the TV off.

'Come on, Allie,' Dad said. 'We were watching that.'

'I need to talk to you both.'

Right away they looked worried, and I almost decided not to go ahead with it. Then I imagined myself telling Mrs Goodall that I couldn't do it. I didn't want to tell her that.

There was nowhere to sit, so I stayed where I was. I told them that I'd been talking to the counsellor at school, and that she said I needed a clean space of my own to do my VCE work.

I felt sick, ashamed and angry all at once. I'd never spoken to them directly like that about the house.

I know it's strange, but we never talk about it.

Mum got anxious, pulling at her hair, unravelling bits of wool from the old cardigan she wore. Her hands were shaking.

'I can't live like this anymore,' I said. I wasn't going to cry. It would have made Mum feel worse. 'You have to help me.'

'What do you want, love?' Dad asked. His voice was gentle.

I told Dad that I needed money to hire one of those big skips that they put on the nature strip. I told them that I wanted to empty out all the rubbish that had been in my room for years; that I needed a clear space for my clothes and books.

Mum wouldn't look at me. 'It's not that bad,' she muttered, almost to herself, but I didn't answer.

I told them I was going to ask Uncle Leo to come the next day to help. It had to be Saturday because I worked at Hungry Jacks on Sundays.

Mum nodded, but I could tell she hated the idea.

THAT AFTERNOON, I ordered the biggest skip you could get and I told them we'd need it for a week.

THEY BROUGHT it very early this morning. It was huge. Mum hid in the house, but Dad went out and spoke to the men in the truck. He showed them where to put it, and gave them the money.

Then Uncle Leo and Trent arrived.

'Wow, big skip, Allie,' Uncle Leo said as he hugged me. 'How're you doing, Harry? Where's Bernie?'

Dad nodded towards the house.

'Not coping?'

'No.'

WE WORKED ALL DAY. I'd bought rolls of those really tough rubbish bags, the ones you were supposed to use in the garden. I was embarrassed for Uncle Leo and Trent to see my room, but I had to put up with it if we were going to get anything done. They just got to work.

Trent was big and strong. He carried the heavy bags to the skip when they were full. I couldn't believe how much stuff we packed up and threw away. There was every kind of rubbish that Mum and Dad had collected over eighteen years. Well, Mum collected it really; Dad just didn't stop her.

Everything you could imagine!

Ancient newspapers in high piles, magazines, store catalogues and every other kind of junk mail going back years; old shoes, many of them Mum's from her childhood; boxes and boxes of Christmas and birthday cards, every one she'd ever received; every item of my clothing from the time I was a baby; broken toys; all of my paintings and drawings, beginning with kinder and then right through primary school; wrapping paper years old; hundreds of letters; craft supplies she's never used; mouldy paperbacks and every book she'd ever owned; a collapsible bird bath; a roasting pan big enough to cook two turkeys; broken dolls and prams; my baby cradle; a portable cot; a change table she must have used when I was a baby; at least twenty packets of disposable nappies; a broken sewing machine, and old sewing patterns not even opened.

That was just some of it.

We sorted out the stuff we could give to the Salvos, and packed all the rest into garbage bags. One by one they went to the skip. The neighbours had a good look. There must have been fifty bags in the skip by the time we finished clearing everything out.

Mum fluttered around for half an hour or so, making a funny noise, like a cat mewling. She couldn't bear seeing her stuff thrown away. I was sure she thought I was betraying her, and to be honest, it did feel like a betrayal, but I had to do it.

Uncle Leo stepped in, saying, 'Bernie, it might be better if you go do something else. There are enough of us here to help Alison. I know it's hard for you.'

So Mum went off talking to herself in the way she did, and hid in her room for the rest of the day. Dad stayed.

Finally we could see the floor, nice dark-coloured boards, still shiny. Soon I had a cupboard where I could store my clothes, and we had cleared the rubbish off my dresser. The room looked big.

There was a book I loved when I was small. I didn't remember the story, but I kept the book under my pillow and took it out often just to stare at one picture. It was of a little girl in a big bedroom. It was an old-fashioned book. You could tell by the furniture in the room, and by the frilly nightdress, and the little white cap the girl wore in bed. I think they called them 'mob caps'. Her bed was very high and wide. There were lots of soft-looking pillows and a pale blue and grey-striped eiderdown.

The thing I loved best about the picture was the big armchair at the end of the bed. All of her clothes for the next day were folded neatly on the chair, waiting for her. There was a long dress with a sash, a shawl, a petticoat with flounces, white stockings and, on the floor, small, shiny red boots. Everything was perfect, clean and ordered. The girl sat in her bed, safe and cared for, reading a storybook. Tucked in next to her was an old-fashioned doll, the kind with skin that looked like china.

The picture filled me with wonder. I wanted to be that little girl. I would stare at her for a long time, imagining what it would be like to sleep in that big, neat bedroom, with all the books and toys I wanted, and with pretty, clean clothes waiting for me.

I knew that this was a 'fantasy' for me, but at least I had a clean room now. I smiled brightly for the first time in … well … I couldn't remember when.

. . .

I WAS SWEEPING the floor later that day, and Trent was cleaning the window, when Uncle Leo said, 'I've got something I think you can use, Allie.'

He went back to his house and returned half an hour later with a small desk that he took from the back of his car. It was made from warm red-gold-brown polished wood. Uncle Leo told me that it was rosewood, and that it was an antique, made in the 1850s. It had belonged to his mother, my grandmother.

I didn't know anything about furniture, but I could see that it was valuable. The lid sloped gently down, just right for reading or using a laptop. Under the lid there was room to store books, stationery, pens, anything you needed. At the back left corner there was a hole containing a funny little cup. Uncle Leo explained that it was an ink well. He said that when he was small he would watch his mother filling her fountain pen from it. The fountain pen was special. She used it to write letters, answer invitations or send cards. Sometimes, he told me, she'd let him sit on her lap as she wrote in her flowing writing. He told me that the smell of the ink combined with his mother's perfume was one of his happiest memories from his childhood.

Most amazing were the legs. They were curled like your hair when you used an electric curler; just like ringlets. More than 160 years ago, someone had carved them from a piece of wood, then planed and polished them until they were perfect. On the left side of the desk were four drawers, so that when you were sitting at it you just had to reach around to the side to get anything you needed. I could keep envelopes, paper clips, a stapler, even my diary there. On the other side was a small cabinet with a fancy latch. There was not a mark or scratch on the desk.

It was the loveliest thing I had ever seen. I wanted it so badly. I couldn't wait to unpack everything from my school bag and put it all away. Then it would be mine, as well as my grandmother's.

Uncle Leo put the desk in place under the window.

'It's time you had something of hers.' He put his arm around my shoulders and drew me close. 'She'd love you to have it. You're very like her in many ways.'

'How?'

'Oh, you have her amazing blue eyes and her colouring. She had thick, brown hair like you. And you have a kind heart like her.'

I had to look away and swallow hard. No one had ever told me that.

EVERYTHING WAS SWEPT, dusted and cleaned. I'd taken the curtains down to wash them, and the window sparkled. I could see across the weeds in the backyard to the park where children played on the swings. Dad had disappeared as he often did. Uncle Leo and Trent were about to leave, but they were coming back to paint my room the next day while I was at work.

Suddenly, Mum was in the doorway. I didn't know how long she'd been there. She looked terrible. Her hair was sticking up everywhere, and her face and eyes were puffy. She stared at the desk. 'Mummy's desk,' she whispered.

'Yes, Bern.' Uncle Leo's voice was very gentle. 'I've given it to Alison.'

'Give it to me, give it to me.' Her voice wasn't a whisper anymore; it was a shriek. She went to the desk and touched it, and then she got down on her knees awkwardly and put her arms around it, caressing it as if it was alive.

'Give it to me, it's mine,' she cried again.

Uncle Leo stooped down to her. 'Bern, you've got lots of Mum's things.'

Did she? Where were they? Were they buried somewhere under everything else?

'Alison doesn't have anything of Mum's, and she needs a desk for her study.'

Mum was crying, keening in that desolate way, as if the most terrible thing in the world had happened to her. For a strange moment, I watched her as if I'd never met her before. She was very overweight. Then my love and compassion flooded back.

'Mummy used to let me fill the inkwell,' she wailed. She stayed kneeling in front of the desk for about five minutes.

Uncle Leo held up open hands to Trent and me. 'Let her be.'

When she quietened a little, I said, 'I'll look after it, I promise, Mum.'

She let me kiss her on the cheek, and then she got up stiffly and stumbled for the door, crying loudly.

Trent had been watching everything. 'Look,' he said. 'I'm going to the café down the street to get some coffees. Alison, why don't you put your things in your desk, and Leo and your mum and me will have a coffee before we go.'

I LOVE MY MUM, but I know that she's sick.

I knew that losing her mother made her want to die too. I also knew that when I wasn't there, Mum would be in my room, looking through the desk, putting things in it. She would probably try to move it into her room and find a place for it on top of all the other stuff.

I rang Dad. He was at either the pub or the TAB. 'I need you to come home, Dad. And on the way can you call in at the hardware store. Get me a latch for the outside of my bedroom door and a padlock with a key.'

Dad was quiet for a few seconds. 'I dunno love, do you really have to go that far?'

'You know I do. Please.'

'Okay,' he sighed, 'be home soon.'

I was very tired, but I looked around that big, clean room and felt strong. What Mrs Goodall said was true; the only one who could change my life was me. I couldn't take my eyes off the desk. I imagined my grandmother sitting at it, writing letters, her long, dark hair falling over her shoulders. The desk was something beautiful from the past, something that connected me to her.

Then the guilt flooded in …

What kind of heartless bitch have you become, Alison?

CHAPTER 8

BERNADETTE BRENNAN

SUNDAY, 21 FEBRUARY

'Mousy,' Daddy had said. 'She's a mousy little thing.'

They didn't know I was listening back then.

'You have to stop her clinging to you, Mary.'

Mousy. I watched a mouse once. It poked its head out of a tiny hole in the corner of the kitchen. Its little nose twitched, and it looked around to see if it was safe. Then it ran along the floor close to the wall. It stopped to pick up a slither of apple skin, and it stood there concentrating, nibbling the food with its tiny pink paws up to its face. I stayed still. I didn't want it to go. A noise at the door. It darted back to its hole and disappeared.

I'm mousy, Daddy says. Yes, I'm like that mouse. I'll only leave my hole when it's safe.

Leo and I used to mess around with this game. It went — Bernadette Brennan, the universe, the Milky Way, the solar system, Earth, the Southern Hemisphere, Australia, Melbourne, Toorak, 20 Marlin Grove, my bedroom, my bed, my body.

The last four were my world, sometimes just the last three.

My body was the final fence. My bed protected it. My bedroom was safe, but not always the house, and never outside.

But there was a time when my body didn't feel safe, and my bedroom was a place of horror and pain.

When I turned twenty-one, Mummy and Daddy gave me a pearl necklace — big gleaming globes, perfectly round, with a soft, pinky sheen. Mummy said they came from Broome. So big and round. Too precious to wear.

'Don't lose them,' Daddy said. 'You know what you're like.'

It was a hot, hot night. I woke up with cramps like a knife in my stomach, my pelvis hard like concrete, unbearable, and something pushing, pushing, trying to get out. The bed was wet. I must have cried out because Mummy was there.

'What darling, what?'

Cool hand on my forehead. My stomach was hard between breaths, between gasps, crying, snot running down. She put her hand there.

'No, no! Oh my God, no. Darling no.'

Then it was out with a *whoosh*, slithery like a fish. A red, blue, purple thing came out from between my legs, dead, streaked with white filmy stuff. I couldn't look. *No. Take it away. Take it.*

It would go to 'Limbo'. The nuns at school told us that that was what happened to babies who died without baptism.

Mummy's voice was gentle now. 'It's a boy. Dead.' She flicked water from my glass onto its forehead.

'I baptise you …' Then she made the sign of the triangular God on its purple head. 'I baptise you,' she said softly with love.

'One more push,' she then urged, 'get the rest out.'

Then the livery thing slurped out, and she covered them both with the sheet, the dead boy and its placenta. There was blood now, and mess, all sticky, and the baby was dead.

She took it all away, the purple baby and the livery thing. I lay in my mess — sleep was coming and going. Had I dreamt it?

No, there she was again, everything gone, a bowl of warm water, soap, towels, clean sheets. She washed me, smoothed my hair back from my face, clean now, but leaking blood. She gave me a pill and water. 'Sleep now, we won't tell anyone; it's morning soon, don't get up.'

I didn't get up, not for weeks. Mummy must have told Daddy something. He wasn't curious. My flesh folded around me like a coat. I was glad I was big. It was somewhere to hide. She came to my room every day, with soup and sandwiches and small white pills that I swallowed with sweet tea. I slept.

Only once did she take my face and turn it to her. 'Who Bernadette? Who did it?'

I didn't say. He told me not to. Pushed my head back against the bedhead.

Don't tell, don't tell, don't tell.

'We're going, Bernadette. Come on.'

We were going to visit Mummy in hospital, the first time she was there when we still thought she'd get better. He was waiting. I stepped out of the front door and then I was falling. I grabbed the heavy doorknob. My heart pounded in my chest, my face sweating.

I'm going to die.

'Hurry up,' Daddy yelled.

I couldn't move. *Going to vomit. I can't move, I can't move.* No breath. Shaking.

'What's wrong with you?'

Pressure was in my head and neck. My eyes couldn't focus.

The world belongs to everyone else but me. I'm not in it, a bystander. I can't get through the membrane into the world where Daddy dangles the car keys, waiting.

'I'm sick.' I stepped back into the house and crept up to my bedroom. Soon my heart would burst out of my chest.

Lying on the bed, shaking and terrified. *Breathe, breathe.* Down under the quilt, I hid.

I heard the car leave.

Daddy's disgusted when he looks at me. I'm fat. I hide in my fat. It's like the hole the mouse peeped out of. If there's something scary, I can scurry back inside.

LEO GAVE Alison Mummy's desk. Then she put that big lock on her door. She won't let me go into her room. I just want to look at Mummy's desk. When I was small I'd sit on the floor underneath it with my doll. It was a little nest. I'd trace the pattern on the carpet and put my face against Mummy's legs.

'They threw away my things, Harry. Can you go out there and bring them back?' I demanded.

'It's Alison's room,' he said.

Just that.

Then after a minute, he said, 'She's talking to the counsellor at school, and that bloke and sheila from Child Protection are hanging around. They might take her away.'

CHAPTER 9

TRENT GRIERSON

SUNDAY, 21 FEBRUARY

I'D SHOWERED, PUT ON CLEAN CLOTHES, AND RUBBED MY HANDS with sanitiser, but the smell still drifted around me, a smell of rotting food and mould. I slumped into a kitchen chair.

'I'm knackered,' I said with a sigh. I wanted to get up and get a beer, but even that seemed too hard.

'Yeah, me too,' Leo agreed, walking over to sit opposite me.

'Her bedroom looked good though. The white paint was a good choice.' I was really happy with what we had accomplished for Alison.

'Yeah, but I think you got more paint in your hair and beard than you did on the walls.' Leo gently reached over to flick my hair.

'Well, you know, I'm a cop not an interior decorator. Do you want to eat?' I was famished but didn't know if I could find the energy to put ingredients together into a meal.

'Yeah, something quick and easy.'

'I'll make a pasta.' I pulled myself up off the chair and went to the fridge and peered inside.

'What kind of sauce? Tomato, mushroom or cheese?'

'Mushroom if we have enough.'

'There's enough. Here, can you chop this onion?' I knew he was probably too tired to move too, but we had to eat.

He eased himself up off the chair, saying, 'No problem, but on second thoughts, after cleaning out that fridge, I don't know if I can ever look at food again. It was all off. I had to hold my breath as I threw it into bags. It was slimy. The fridge was an incubator for cockroaches. I cleaned it out with disinfectant and a scrubbing brush, then I sprayed surface spray everywhere, but it really needs a professional pest control team. I don't want to think about the oven.'

'Yeah, it was a massive, filthy job. Anyway, I'm going to have a beer. What about you?'

'Is there any of that Shiraz left?' It was his favourite.

'I think so. I'll get you a glass.'

'Amazing that we filled that big skip.'

I poured his wine, gave him a full well-deserved glass. 'I know. While you were doing the fridge, Harry helped me chuck in the stuff that was lying around the front yard.'

'Did he? I'm surprised. I wasn't sure whether he noticed the mess or not.'

'You wouldn't believe it. Old bikes, kids' tricycles, half a dog kennel, rusted car parts, bits of wire fencing, a wrecked barbecue, broken chairs, an old TV set, every kind of junk you could imagine.' I shivered at the thought of all the rubbish.

'Maybe now he can mow the grass and weeds.'

'If he can find a mower in that shed that works. It looks worse than the house.' I still couldn't get over the amount of junk we had to move. 'I can't help wondering, though, Leo,' I said as I handed him his glass of wine. 'Is this really the way to go about it? Doing it for them, I mean. We know it will be just as bad in a few months' time. When are they going to take responsibility themselves?'

'I don't think either of them is capable of that. Bernie

needs help, but can you imagine her agreeing to get it. So she'll keep on surrounding herself with stuff, as a way to hide. And Harry won't do anything to upset her.'

'Where does that leave Alison?' The anger I'd been feeling all day made me raise my voice. 'She has rights. It's not legal to make a kid live like that. They should be charged with child neglect and abuse. It's not your responsibility to dig them out, but I'm an officer of the law. I have a duty to put in a complaint to the Department of Human Services.'

'Please don't do that, Trent.'

But I couldn't just let it go. 'How does not complaining help Alison?'

'They'd take her away to a foster home. I don't see dobbing them in as the way to go. She'd hate seeing her parents in trouble. I think there's a better way to do it. Alison needs people in her life who can support her in taking charge. She's talking to that counsellor and that's paid off. At least now she has a clean, private room of her own. I figure we can help her to change little things. Bernie and Harry won't do it.'

'What do you mean?'

'Well after I scrubbed out the fridge, I told her to try to take charge of what went in and out of it. She can make a list of fruit, vegies, groceries, and meat every week, and she can give it to Harry. That's the least he can do, go to the supermarket for food. I'm going to give her a cookbook of simple, healthy recipes that she can cook for them, instead of phoning for that disgusting takeaway they live on.'

'That's a lot of responsibility to put on a kid who's trying to do Year Eleven.'

'I know, but Alison's strong. Did you see how determined she was to get that room cleared out yesterday? And the fuss over Mum's desk. She got a lock for the door.'

'Yeah, I wanted to cheer her for that.'

I went outside to pick basil for the pasta sauce. Chester

was whingeing at the door, and as soon as I opened it he darted inside and ran around in circles in excitement.

'Feed him please, Leo, before he wrecks the place.'

Leo sighed and took Chester and his food out to the veranda.

I knew he didn't want to talk about it, but I couldn't leave it alone. So when he came back in, I said, 'Look, I know Alison's strong, but my point is, why should she have to be? She's a sixteen-year-old girl. She should have boyfriends. She should be wasting time with other kids, bringing them home. She should be able to come home from school knowing there'll be a healthy meal, food in the fridge. She shouldn't need to take her clothes, sheets and towels to a laundromat at the weekends. She shouldn't have to go to the gym for a shower. She should be able to depend on her parents to give her the basics. She should have a social life for God's sake.'

Leo was silent.

I was worked up. 'I know we got her room done, but the rest of the house? She can cook all the healthy meals she likes, but there's nowhere to eat. The table's piled high with years of junk. And to cook anything, she'd need to clear and clean the stovetop, and the oven, not to mention finding and scrubbing pots, pans, plates, and cutlery. It's a big job.'

Leo sipped his wine while I served the pasta, and then said, 'Yes, I know all of that. But not every kid lives in an ideal family. I can't change the situation she lives in, but I can have faith in her, and encourage her to try to change it in little ways. Let her know that we're there for her. Incidentally, have you seen how Harry will do anything she asks. She needs to get him more on side.'

Harry has a lot to answer for, I thought. At certain times during the long afternoon, I'd wanted to shake him until his teeth rattled in his head.

Leo ate his pasta, apparently forgetting he wasn't hungry.

'Fantastic pasta, Trent. I just want to get her through to leaving school and going to uni. Then she can move out.'

'She could stay here with us.'

'She'd never agree. Bernie would see it as rejection, a judgment on her. Alison wouldn't hurt her that much.'

'What is it with Bernie? How did she get like this?'

'My understanding's patchy. She had some kind of nervous breakdown when she was twenty-one, stayed in bed for weeks. It was at the time when I was having a lot of problems myself, trying to be a model son for the Judge. Then as she seemed to be recovering, I went to the clinic and then to India. When I came home she was virtually a prisoner in the house, wouldn't go out anywhere unless Mum dragged her. Then she'd be likely to have a panic attack.'

'Has she had help?'

'Yes. When Mum was alive she had regular appointments with a psychiatrist, but she fell apart when Mum died. She didn't even visit Mum in hospital. Couldn't go out the front door.' He shook his head.

'After your mother's death, I can imagine what it must have been like for her in that house with the Judge.'

Leo looked baffled by these memories. 'She just got worse and worse. The Judge more or less ignored her.'

'I don't get it, Leo. I mean, you came through your own breakdown and you're one of the most mentally healthy people I've ever met. What happened to her?'

'Bernie was always very vulnerable, I don't really know why.'

'She's like a frightened animal.'

We took a glass of wine each into the living room, and Chester settled on the couch with me. I suggested that we might watch *Sixty Minutes*, but neither of us could be bothered.

'What's Harry's story?' I asked.

'I honestly don't know. He never talks about himself. Never talks full stop.'

'He seems sort of, I don't know the word, a bit slow,' I remarked. 'I can't fathom how he can let his daughter live in that place.'

Leo nodded before taking a big sip of his wine. 'Yes, I know what you mean. When he worked for Dad at the house in Toorak, there wasn't anything he couldn't do with his hands, and he was a whiz in the garden. But I always thought there was a bit of brain damage. He couldn't hold a conversation, and couldn't look you in the eye.'

'How on earth did he end up with Bernie?'

'Well, think about it.' Leo stood and opened the door to let Chester out for his nightly sniff around the garden. 'Mum's gone. Bernie's terrified of the Judge. She wants to get out of that house but can't because her phobia keeps her trapped inside. Harry's kind to her, gradually convinces her to come out to the garden, stays beside her, supports her. Now she has someone else to cling to. He's older than her, and she can lean on him. She wouldn't have needed much convincing to go away with him, and then let the Judge know after the fact.'

'But the Judge rescued them, didn't he?'

'In a way. He had to come in and take over as usual. He bought that house for them, and he gives her an allowance. Harry still gets a little bit of work every now and then, but most of the time he just looks after Bernie.'

'What about Alison?' I was on a roll and needed to learn as much as I could about this perplexing family.

'She was born in their second year together. You know, Trent, the place was always messy, although not as bad as it is now. But the two of them genuinely love Alison. In their own way they did everything they could for her. Harry would play with her for hours. They took her to playgroups, and to kinder and later to school. But things deteriorated when she was at primary school. It was so bad at one stage that one of the neighbours got the Department to check on Alison's safety.'

'What happened?'

'They were given two weeks to fix the place up or Alison was going into care. Bernie was hysterical. I went and helped them clear it out; it really did take two weeks. So they avoided losing her then, but it's always on their minds. Any day they know the Department could turn up. They must be terrified that she's talking to this counsellor at school.'

'Thank God she's talking to someone.'

CHAPTER 10
COLIN BRENNAN
FRIDAY, 25 MARCH

She arrived on the 3.15pm train from Melbourne, and stepped onto the platform looking for me.

A smile of recognition broke across her face, and she came towards me through the crowd of people alighting and boarding. For a breath-taking moment it was 1955, and I was watching Mary come to me across the library quadrangle at Melbourne University. I couldn't speak. She had the same startling blue eyes, the same luxuriant, dark brown hair, the poised bearing of someone moving through the world untouched by its ugliness.

It was Alison, grown into a young woman, and dressed in jeans, light blue checked shirt and sandals for the warm day. I felt tears, and struggled to disguise them. I wouldn't be a maudlin old fool.

I bent to kiss her and took her heavy school bag.

'You look well, Grandpa,' she said, slipping her arm through mine as if it hadn't been four years since we'd seen each other.

I was overcome and foolishly full of pride to have this lovely young woman, my granddaughter, walking arm in arm with me. In my vanity, I hoped we'd see someone I knew. I wanted to show her off.

'You've brought school work,' I commented as we loaded her heavy school bag, laptop and backpack into the car.

'Yes, lots of assignments, but there'll still be time for the beach.'

On the drive back to Golden Beach, I filled the air with small talk like a nervous adolescent, but she seemed not to notice that I was chattering. She had the same self-containment I had recognised in her when she was small. She had made her own world, of necessity I suppose, and she would relate to everyone from her firm ground within it. There were secrets she would not give away. I found it both admirable and sad that she had needed to build this carapace.

At the house, without bothering about her bags, she was up the stairs and across the room to look out at the sea. She opened the window and the wash of brine and seaweed, the thunder of breakers, the squawking of seagulls flooded in.

'Oh, there are lots of people on the beach.'

It was Good Friday, the beginning of the school holidays, and perhaps the last stretch of sunshine before winter. There were beach umbrellas, little ones in those melanoma-proof bathers they wore these days, dogs, a few hopefuls waiting for an early evening bite, and kites sailing high in a gusty wind. I wished I could keep forever the image of her slim figure and strong back framed against the sunlit window.

CHAPTER 11
ALISON BRENNAN
FRIDAY, 25 MARCH

GRANDPA LOOKED GOOD. HIS HAIR WAS STILL THICK AND whiter than ever. He had a high forehead, which made him look distinguished. He was more slumped in the shoulders though. Well, I should have expected that, as he was about eighty years old.

As soon as I'd dumped my bags, I went across to the beach. I sat and wriggled my toes in the sand, watching the waves come in. A big, muscular dog ran up to me, but it only wanted to sniff and play. I patted its head and scratched its ears until its owner called it away. I watched a seagull soaring up high. It seemed to be sailing on the wind. Along the beach two boys flew kites. Higher and higher they climbed as the boys ran and called to each other.

It must be awesome to fly, to feel the wind hold you up, to slide and dip on it like on a rollercoaster. I imagined just leaving everything and climbing into the air.

When I talked to Mrs Goodall yesterday, she gave me a sheet of paper and a texta and asked me to draw two concentric circles. Then she asked me to draw a symbol of myself right at the centre of the circles. I was thinking about coming here to the beach the next day, so I drew a seagull. She asked me why I chose a seagull, and I said because it could go anywhere, it was free; it could climb high in the clean air. Mrs Goodall said it was a good symbol for me. I was like a bird that needed to get free of a cage.

Then she asked me to put around the inner circle all the people I could rely on for support and help. So I put her, then Grandpa, and Leo and Trent, and finally Dad. I didn't put Mum, although I would have if I were doing this even a few months ago. Mum was still on my side then. Mrs Goodall asked me why there were no friends of my own age in the circle. I had to explain that it was too hard for me to have friends. I couldn't bring them to my house — they'd die of disgust.

'But do you have to bring them to your house?' she asked. 'Couldn't you go out at the weekends, be together at lunchtime, study together in the library? You might find there are girls and boys who also have problems at home, maybe even problems like yours. No one has a perfect family.'

Then she asked me to put in the outer circle all the other things that helped me, not people this time, but hobbies, and other things that I enjoyed. So I put my sport, of course, my gym workouts and being on the swimming team. I put books, because I loved reading.

She asked me if I would consider looking for support online. She gave me the address of a blog run by children of hoarders. She said that she'd been following it for a while and she thought it would help me. 'Another forum of support, maybe,' she said.

As the day began to cool, I retraced those circles on the sand, and thought about that seagull, and opening the door of my cage little by little.

Only a month or so ago it seemed impossible that I would ever be able to get out of that house. But there were little rays of light. I was opening the cage bit by bit. Clearing out my room was the first, then getting Grandma's desk. Then coming here to spend the holidays with Grandpa.

I told Dad first that I was going to Grandpa's, and he was cool, but I knew what Mum's reaction would be, so I had left it until the day before.

'Oh, by the way, Mum, I'm going to Grandpa's house for the holidays,' I had announced her to.

She stared at me with a horrified expression, as if she was the child and I was the adult abandoning her. After the weekend when we cleared out my room, she didn't get out of bed for a week. I brought her tea and food, but she wouldn't look at me. She'd be in bed now, burrowing in, nursing her hurt feelings, telling herself that she was a failure, that I didn't love her, that she didn't deserve me.

I do love Mum, I always have. But she thinks love means being like her, giving in to her. She thinks that if I love her, I won't try to break out, to have a life. Everything I do to change my life and build a future for myself upsets her, but I have to try, otherwise my life will be just as horrible as hers.

I was tracing the circles on the sand, thinking about all of that when Grandpa found me. Quickly, I brushed the circles away.

'Ready to eat?'

I was starving.

So we walked back to the house. Grandpa was going to cook fish; of course, it was Good Friday.

Grandpa's very religious; I must remember that.

I didn't know much about religion, although I was baptised and I made my First Communion and Confirmation in primary school. Mum and Dad didn't go to church — another failure of their parenting, Grandpa probably thought.

I made a salad to go with the fish, using tomatoes and lettuce from Grandpa's garden, with avocado and lemon juice. Grandpa steamed new potatoes and fried the fish in butter. It was delicious. We didn't talk much, there was no need — we were both introverts.

After dinner, he sat in front of the TV, and then I wandered down to the store for an ice-cream. There were people everywhere, eating fish and chips, and kids playing in the park next to the beach. There was a lot of activity around a caravan parked outside the store. There was a fishing competition and this was where the fish were weighed and judged. I ate my ice-cream and felt very relaxed, almost happy.

Back at the house I set up my laptop and found the blog Mrs Goodall had told me about. There were hundreds of pages, written by kids in the same situation as me. I was reading my life. I began to copy pieces and saved them in a new document. I wanted to build up a picture, to get a wider perspective on my situation, as Mrs Goodall would have said.

This was the first thing I saved.

While hoarding appears most dramatically to be about 'stuff', to a child of a hoarder, it's really about relationships, family dynamics, shame, and self-worth. Many children of hoarders have been conditioned — consciously or otherwise — to believe that they are less important than things.

The words underlined themselves in my head: shame, self-worth, stuff more important. Yes, that was the feeling — that Mum cared more about her stuff than about me. She should have cared that I couldn't bring people to the house. She should have cared that we couldn't eat a meal at the table or cook in the kitchen because of the cockroaches. She should have cared that I couldn't shower at home, that the house stunk, and that I had to lock my bedroom to keep a private space for myself.

I was resentful, and it was a different feeling from what I had before. Then I was just filled with sadness for her. I didn't want to hurt her. I wanted to protect her and help her keep her secret. But now I was beginning to see that my life was important too, and that her stuff shouldn't be more important than me.

Things were beginning to change for me. Before now, I forgave Mum for everything. I loved her in that helpless kind of way you had when you were a little kid. You didn't know what to do — you were stuck.

Now I could see that there were other people and things that mattered. I didn't know if I could go on forgiving her for the rest of her life.

I'd bought a copy of Sonya Hartnett's *Golden Boys* the day before, and I was longing to read it. I took a shower, called goodnight to Grandpa and went to bed with the book. Tomorrow I'd make a timeline for completing the assignments. The sound and smell of the ocean blew in the open window.

CHAPTER 12
ALISON BRENNAN
SUNDAY, 10 APRIL

THE TWO WEEKS WERE LIKE A LATE SUMMER. I SPENT HOURS reading and walking on the beach, and watching the waves barrelling in from Bass Strait. When Uncle Leo came to visit, I played with Chester on the beach. I threw a ball and he raced furiously to pick it up, and then he stood covered in sand, wagging his tail, refusing to give up the ball until I prised it from his mouth. Chester made me laugh. We had a barbecue lunch in the garden that day and there was no sign of old 'Mr Grumble Bum', as Uncle Leo called Grandpa behind his back. Perhaps it helped that Trent was working that day and couldn't be there.

Grandpa was kind to me, but not in a pushy or smothering way. He showed me photos of my grandmother, and she was just as lovely as Uncle Leo had said. Grandpa also told me I was like her, and I looked for signs of myself in her straight figure, in her hair and her smile. There were photos of their wedding, old, faded, black and whites, and lots of photos of Grandma with the children.

Mum was a shy, blonde girl clinging to her mother, and Leo was a sturdy boy, looking straight into the camera. There was a beautiful photo of their first car, a Dodge Wayfarer

Grandpa said, which they bought in 1958, just after they were married. It was a big, shiny, black car, sleek and handsome. Grandpa sat proudly in the driver's seat and Grandma, wearing a navy blue suit, with a navy hat and white gloves, stood beside the car waving at the camera. Grandpa couldn't stop looking at the photo.

'She was lovely,' I said.

'Yes, she was a lovely car,' he said.

'I meant Grandma,' I said, and we both laughed.

I didn't think about Mum and Dad much over those two weeks. I worked through my assignments and followed the blog Mrs Goodall had told me about. Sometimes very early in the morning I sat on the sand while Grandpa fished, and in the evenings we walked together to the store for ice-creams, eating them as we watched the children in the park.

On the last day of the holidays, when Grandpa drove me to the station in Sale, I held my tears back.

'Come again soon, dear girl,' he said as he kissed me.

Then I was on the train, with a nervous ache in my stomach, and three hours to prepare myself for what I would find at home.

I felt sick as I drew nearer to the house. The front yard was worse than ever; the junk that Trent had thrown into the skip seemed to have come back and multiplied ten times. The front door wasn't locked, but there were piles of papers and boxes wedged behind it. I sent them skittering as I forced my bags and myself through. I climbed over the rubbish in the front room, slipping and sliding, trying to get a footing. The path I had tried to clear through it all before I left had disappeared.

I almost turned away, to run back to Golden Beach, to run anywhere.

I don't know if I can do this anymore, I thought.

All the way home in the train I had imagined finding my room violated, the lock broken, Grandma's desk gone, and

Mum's junk covering every surface, so I was relieved to see that the padlock was still intact.

I opened the door with my key. The room was as neat as I'd left it. I dropped my bags, opened the window and turned to face the rest of the house.

Slipping on the stuff underfoot, I made my way to Mum and Dad's room, calling to them as I went. The smell was even worse than I remembered, but I couldn't open any windows without moving the piles of stacked rubbish, papers, boxes, bits and pieces of furniture, and strange, useless objects.

I hadn't spoken to Mum for two weeks. She didn't answer her phone when I rang and she ignored my messages and texts. Perhaps her phone was lost in the mess.

I found her in her bedroom. Bottles of pills littered the floor. She'd been shopping online, for there were packets of new purchases, many unopened, piled up around her on the floor and the bed. With the stuff that was already there, the additional new piles made the room look like one of those out of control stalls you saw at flea markets.

I couldn't see Mum, but her shape was there, buried under the bedclothes. The smell was especially bad in this room, a mixture of sweat, urine, unwashed hair and dirty bedding. There were plates of half eaten stale food everywhere, and remains of cups of tea with milk congealed on the surface.

I began to retch, and had to run back to the open window in my bedroom to breathe in some clean air. When I came back into Mum's room, I pushed a pile of stuff aside and forced the window open.

'Close it,' she screamed from under the piles of blankets.

'No, it stays open. I'm going to get some air into this stinking place.' I went closer and bent to kiss her, but she pushed me away roughly. Her face was white and puffy. Her hair was a mass of greasy, knotted, grey curls, and her finger-nails, where she clutched the bedclothes, were black. Her eyes were glazed. What pills was she taking?

'Why are you in bed, Mum?' I asked. 'Are you sick? Where's Dad?'

'Don't know where he is.'

'Have you tried his phone?'

'Nooooo …' she drew the word out and burrowed down further.

I didn't know what to do. 'Mum, this is awful. The house is worse than ever. How long since you got out of bed?'

Suddenly she turned on me. 'What do you care, traitor? You couldn't care less about me. You threw my stuff away in that bin, and took my mother's desk. Then you ran off to that cruel old man's place and left me here. I suppose the two of you have been talking about me these last two weeks. You don't love me. It was just pretence.'

'You know I love you, Mum,' I protested.

'If you loved me you'd stay when I need you. I thought I could rely on you, but you left me like everyone else. Well, you cast me off so you can go too. Go on, get out, you think you're too good for this house.'

The unfairness of her attack winded me. She was snarling, vicious. I noticed that her teeth were streaked with yellow and green plaque. Hygiene had been abandoned, probably on the day I left. She had turned in on herself, choosing to hide inside her layers of skin as an animal curled up to lick its wounds. Yet despite her crazy fury, I still felt the old ache of helpless, hopeless love and pity. I cleared a place on the bed and sat down, reaching for her hand.

'I'm home now, Mum. Let's get you out of bed and we'll fill some buckets so you can have a wash. Then we'll get something to eat and I'll help you change the sheets on your bed.'

'No, go away! Leave me alone. I don't need you. He's gone and you can go too.'

'Come on, Mum, you'll feel much better. I'll wash your hair for you. We can eat and then watch some TV.'

'Can't wash, there's no water,' she muttered.

The nausea rose in my stomach again. 'What's wrong with the water?'

'There hasn't been any water for over a week.'

What now? Was it an unpaid bill, or a fault with the plumbing? Where was Dad?

'Well, we'll have to get a plumber in. We can't live here without water.'

She began to shriek again, striking out at me with her fists. A wave of her foul body odour washed over me.

'No, no, no one's coming here. We can manage. You can buy bottles of drinking water.'

If the situation wasn't so desperate, I could almost have laughed. She really believed that we could live in this filthy place without water. I knew then that she needed much more help than I was able to give her. I couldn't carry it anymore. I had to ask for help if I was to save myself, and not be sucked into the mental and physical mire in which she lived.

I left her crying in her room, and feeling sick in my stomach, I looked around the rest of the house. There was the usual swarm of cockroaches in the kitchen, feasting on the grease that covered the stovetop, benches and dirty plates, but it was in the bathroom that the nausea finally overcame me. The stench filled my nostrils and seemed to penetrate my skin and hair. I vomited when I saw the overflowing, unflushed toilet whose contents had leaked onto the old newspapers, magazines and wads of tissues and dirty clothing that covered the floor.

'Oh, Mum,' I groaned. I doubled over, heaving again.

I don't know how to help you anymore. Where are you Dad?'

I found wet wipes and a bottle of water in in my backpack. I wiped my face and swished water over my tongue and teeth. Then I took my phone and rang Dad's number.

'The number you have called is not connected. Please check the number and try again …'

I knew now that I had no choice. My desperate voice went

to Uncle Leo's message bank. 'It's Alison. Mum's very bad. I need help. Please, please call me as soon as you can.'

I left the same message in a text and then went back to Mum's room. She was pretending to be asleep. I sat on the bed and took her hand. Uncle Leo would know what to do. I stayed with her until help came.

CHAPTER 13

LEO BRENNAN

SUNDAY, 10 APRIL

I WAS SHOOTING A 65TH WEDDING ANNIVERSARY PARTY IN A gracious old home in Ascot Vale when Alison's message pinged on my phone. The guests were beginning to leave, so I made an appointment with the elderly couple for the next day, packed up my gear and texted: *On my way now* to Alison. She'd never asked me for help before. It must have been bad.

She met me at the door, white faced and looking bilious.

'I can't talk any sense into her. There's no water. The place is disgusting. She won't get out of bed.'

I hadn't seen Bernie since before Alison went to Golden Beach, and I was shocked at her deterioration and at the condition of the house. Worst of all was the smell. I put a hand over my nose and mouth.

'It's the toilet,' Alison said. 'No water. It won't flush.'

'How will she react to me?' I asked.

'She's up and down, screaming one minute and crying the next. She thinks everyone hates her. She's not thinking straight, thinks she can stay here without water.'

This is so unfair on you, Allie, I thought. *Why should you, at sixteen, have to carry this?*

Bernie was hunkered down in her bed, but she raised her head when I came in. I could hardly breathe for the smell, even though a window was open.

'Oh you,' she growled. 'Why are you here? Isn't it enough that you threw out my stuff and gave her Mummy's desk? Now I suppose you've come to stick your nose in again.'

All of Bernie's usual submissiveness had gone and she had become like a hurt animal, lashing out in anger to defend herself.

'Where's Harry, Bernie?'

'Don't know, don't care.'

I cleared a space on the bed and sat next to her. She'd always trusted me, at least until now.

'Let me help you, Bern. You know you can't stay here. Come to my place. You'll be safe there. We can get you clean and get some good food into you.'

That terrified her. She hadn't left the house in over a year. She pushed and hit out at me. She was surprisingly strong. 'No, no, I'm not moving from here, and you can't make me. Go away, go away, and take her too. I can look after myself.'

She began to throw things at me then — empty pill bottles, a TV remote, a bowl full of hairpins. 'Get out, get out,' she screamed.

I knew then that Allie and I couldn't help her. I remembered the name of the psychiatrist who had treated her when she was younger, and I wondered if he was still practising. Outside in front of the house, I downloaded the number. It was Sunday evening, but it was worth a try. The automated message told me that Dr Werstein's hours were nine to five on weekdays, but there was a number for a local Crisis Assessment Team. I rang it.

Please, please come tonight.

. . .

Everything happened quickly after that. There were three of them, calm professionals who took no notice of the state of the house or the smell, who spoke to Bernie with consideration and compassion, despite the fact that she disappeared further under the bedclothes when they came into her room.

'Who are you?' she shrieked? 'Are you from the police? Have you come to take my daughter away?'

Behind me, Alison was sobbing. I put my arm around her and guided her outside the room. 'Get your school things and whatever else you need. You're coming to our place tonight.'

You will never, never spend another night in this house, I vowed silently.

'But Mum?'

'Mum will be going to hospital, she's very sick.'

The medicos had to sedate her. With expert care they moved her onto a stretcher and navigated the obstacles to get her safely into an ambulance.

'Where are you taking her?' I asked.

One of the medicos quickly replied, 'To a psychiatric in-patient clinic at Box Hill. Follow us in your car, please, Sir. There'll be paperwork.'

So I took down the address of the clinic, and then I dropped Alison with her school clothes and books at our house, where Trent was. As I helped her from the car, I said with what I hoped was authority. 'No school for you tomorrow, Allie. Sleep in, and then we'll go back together and get all your stuff. You're not living in that house anymore.'

Her father wasn't there. There was no water, and I was sure there was no food either. It was a squalid and unhealthy place for a teenager.

Alison didn't argue

When I arrived at the clinic, I gave what information I could about Bernie's mental health and her previous treatment. I waited to see her admitted and taken to a private room. She was deep in sedation.

Bernie will never forgive me for this, I thought as I made my way, exhausted, back to Alison and Trent. *Oh God, I'll have to tell the Judge … tomorrow will be soon enough. He can't do anything tonight.*

CHAPTER 14
TRENT GRIERSON
SUNDAY, 10 APRIL

I DIDN'T HAVE MUCH EXPERIENCE WITH TEENAGE GIRLS. GIVE me a room full of coppers any day. But when Leo dropped Alison off at our place, and told me something about the situation, I knew we had to look after her.

In spite of the warmth of the evening, she was shivering. My rudimentary first aid training kicked in, so I wrapped her in a blanket on the couch and brought her a cup of hot chocolate. She took it without a word, staring straight ahead, as if she didn't see me. I couldn't imagine what the events of the evening had been like for her, and what she would have to face in the weeks and months ahead.

She sipped her chocolate and finally managed a smile. 'Thanks, Trent.'

I couldn't help myself, then. I kissed her cheek. 'You're family, love.'

She began to cry, and the gentle sniffling soon became great sobs. I brought her tissues.

'I should never have gone away,' she kept saying, crying and blowing her nose.

Of all the injustices this poor kid has suffered, I thought, *this is surely the worst, that she thinks her mother's condition is her fault.*

'Allie, you can't be expected to take care of your mother 24/7. You have your own life. You have your schoolwork, and you have to think about your future. You had a perfect right to visit your grandfather. You're not to blame. Your mum is in a good place. She'll be well looked after.'

'What's going to happen to her?'

'One day at a time, love. Leo and your grandpa will have to make some decisions until your dad turns up.'

'Where is he, Trent?'

She was confused, like a little child. All of her usual outward confidence had gone.

'I don't know, but I do know this. You're going to stay with us as long as you need.'

I was into comfort food. I had a beef bourgignon pie keeping warm in the oven for Leo, so I cut her a slice and brought it to her on the couch. She was starving. She ate the pie quickly and scraped the bowl with her spoon.

'That was yummy.'

'You must be tired, Allie.'

'Yes, but I'll wait up until Leo gets back to hear about Mum.'

When I went to bed, she and Leo were still talking softly. I left them there together and set my alarm to begin another Monday.

VERY EARLY THE NEXT MORNING, I was jerked awake by the loud ring of my phone. I took it out to the kitchen, although it had probably already woken Leo. It was a police officer from the Flinders Street Precinct.

'There's a suspicious death at Enterprise Park opposite the Casino. We've sent a team of officers down there.'

I knew the park of course. A hangout for shifting groups of homeless and a hotbed of ice distribution.

'What do we know?'

'Not much. A very old man, I believe. Badly bashed.'

'Who called it in?'

'A casino worker on her way home from night shift. She's waiting for you there. Our officers are securing the place and Forensic Services are on the way.'

This wasn't going to be easy. There was a lot of suspicion of police among these homeless communities.

I was pleased that Senior Detective Jocelyn Wallachia's team was rostered on that day. Jossie was the best lead investigator I'd worked with. She was also a great colleague and friend. We were in the same intake at Police Academy, worked at different stations for five or six years, then met up again in detective training. I liked and trusted her.

I rang her, told her what little I knew, and asked her to get her investigating team to the park by seven. I would call my boss when I knew more.

I was desperate for a coffee but I decided to wait and grab a takeaway when I could.

After a quick shower, I threw on a jacket over my jeans and black T-shirt, put on my runners, grabbed my notebook, ID and phone, and jumped into the unmarked police car outside, taking to Melbourne's silent early morning streets.

I parked in King Street and jogged around the back of the Aquarium into Enterprise Park. I could see the entire park, east to west along the north bank of the Yarra, and under the Flinders Street railway bridge. In 1835, Melbourne's first white settlers alighted at this spot from the *Enterprise,* and the annual Melbourne Day was celebrated here.

Across the river I could see the fashionable Southbank Boulevard and Crown Casino, deserted at this early hour. The park had always been a gathering place for Melbourne's increasing homeless population. They clustered around the immense graffiti-covered pylons of the bridge, wrapped in sleeping bags, old doonas and blankets. In the colder weather they set up tents, folding them briefly when the police arrive, only to bring them back in time for the next cold night.

On this morning in early March, the weather was still warm, and there were few tents, but there were several groups congregated together in a jumble of old furniture, couches, tables, milk crates, bicycles, small stoves, tin mugs and plates, as well as piles of blankets and pillows. I saw four of these makeshift communities — bodies huddled together under tarpaulins and blankets.

There were at least a dozen police officers in yellow high-visibility vests protecting the scene, some were standing guard at the entrance to a large cordoned off area, others walked among the park's occupants recording names and keeping lists of anyone who arrived, entered or left the scene.

The body was off by itself, towards the western end of the park, about fifty metres from Aquarium Drive. Outside the cordoned area a young woman, very pale and wrapped in a blanket, was sitting with a female police officer, a cup of steaming liquid in her hand. I walked over and sat next to her, showing my ID to the police officer who identified herself as Constable Bev Talbot.

Then I turned to the young woman. 'Hello, I'm Trent Grierson. I'm a Detective Sergeant with the Homicide Squad. You found the body?'

'Yes, I'm Anna.' She was about twenty, I thought, attractive with a long, thick tawny ponytail and careful make-up. She wore a black cocktail dress, knee-length black raincoat and sneakers. A small backpack, bicycle and helmet were on the ground beside her. She was shaking.

'What time was it when you found the body?'

'Just after five o'clock. It was starting to get light.'

'What were you doing in the park at that time of the morning?'

'I was on my way home.'

'From where?'

'The casino. I'm a croupier. My shift ends at four. I ride my bike across Queens Bridge, through the park and on to Flinders Street to catch the train.'

'Where do you live?'

'Richmond.'

'You said you finished work at four. Why were you an hour later?'

'Usually after work, a group of us goes to an all-night café for breakfast. I start work at eight in the evening. We don't get much of a break to eat. I had breakfast with my friends, and then I was on my way home to sleep. That's where I want to be now.' She began to cry.

The female officer put her arm around her.

'Can you show me where you were when you first saw the body?'

Leaving the blanket on the seat, she walked over to the bike track that linked to Aquarium Drive. Constable Talbot followed.

'I was here.' She stood on a spot perhaps thirty metres north of the body. 'At first I thought he was asleep, but then I realised that he was right out in the open, with no blanket or anything. I stopped my bike and went a bit closer to look. Then I saw his head and all the blood.' She began to cry again.

'This is very important, Anna. Did you touch the body at all?'

She was horrified at the thought. 'No, of course not.'

'You've done everything exactly right,' I said. 'Constable Talbot will take you to the Flinders Street Police Station so you can give a formal statement. When that's all done, you're free to go home. We appreciate your help.' I gave her my card. 'Please contact me immediately if you think of anything else, even if it seems unimportant.'

'What about my bike?'

Constable Talbot answered, 'We've got a police van, Anna. It will fit in the back.'

I SAW the Crime Scene Investigations team make its way towards the cordoned off area. The leader was Sergeant Tim Farange, a cautious and meticulous man. His team of three investigators included a photographer, an exhibits officer and a case file manager. They immediately took charge of the crime scene, and I watched as the photographer began to video and photograph the entire area. The Forensic Pathologist would arrive soon.

I sat on the bench that Anna had vacated and began to fill my notebook with notes about the investigation. I was busy writing when someone came up behind me and waved a cup of rich, dark, aromatic coffee under my nose.

'I thought you'd be hanging for one of these by now.'

It was the fabulous Jossie — friend, colleague, and lead investigator on this case. I told her what little I could at that stage. The residents of the park, awake now, sat in curious groups around its perimeter, talking quietly to each other.

The Forensic Pathologist was Dr Patricia Teasdale, an experienced practitioner of few words. When she arrived, she donned overalls, latex gloves, paper shoes, and a face mask. Then she went to the body to carry out her rituals of swabbing, tape lifts, and temperature taking, the photographer recording every movement.

Jossie and I also put on protective clothing and ducked under the tape to watch as Dr Teasdale did her work. The old man was lying on his right side, and the left side of his skull was almost flattened. Someone strong had done this. The weapon, whatever it was, had battered him over and over again until his skull was a mass of pulped bone and brain.

Trying to hold back revulsion and vomit, I let Dr Teasdale and the photographer do their work. Jossie stepped carefully around the crime scene making notes. Like me, she'd learnt that wallowing in nausea was a distraction. You just had to get on with it.

Apart from the smashed skull, there appeared to be no other injury. The old man was dressed in dirty black trousers, an old-fashioned buttoned shirt and a nylon jacket. He wore cheap, black canvas shoes with no socks.

Dr Teasdale supervised as the man's body was placed on a body bag, and his clothing removed and stored in sealed and labelled bags. She examined the body again, recording comments into a dictaphone. Finally, she covered his head and feet in paper bags and sealed the body bag, just as the contractors arrived to take the remains to the mortuary to await the post mortem.

She then motioned Jossie and me away from the crime scene. 'That's it from me now,' she said, peeling off her face mask, gloves and overalls, and depositing them in a holding bin for processing back at the Forensic Division.

'Talk to me, Patricia.' I needed to know what she'd found.

'As you saw, a very old man, must be in his nineties. Several blows to the side of the head with something heavy. The head trauma is very severe. He's been dead for a few hours. Time of death? Two or three this morning. I'll know more after the autopsy.'

'What about identification? Was there a wallet, health care card, Centrelink card in his clothing? Anything that might tell us who he is?'

'No, nothing. The Crime Scene Investigators might find more. I only looked at the body, but there seem to be some other personal effects over by that pylon.' She pointed to a graffiti-covered pylon one hundred metres or so to the right of the body.

'Okay, thanks Patricia. When will you be able to do the autopsy?'

'As soon as I can this morning, let's say ten o'clock.'

'I'll be there.'

Now it was the turn of the Crime Scene Investigators. They would comb the area, taking samples of footprints, DNA, and photographing blood spatters. They would go through the victim's effects, looking for anything that would identify him. Every tiny piece of potential evidence would be collected.

Finally, Tim Farange came to us. 'Yeah, finished here now. Not much to report. We've bagged up everything, but there's no way to identify him. We're gathering he slept next to that pylon. That's where we found other effects that we're assuming are his — a sleeping bag, pillow and tarp.'

'Nothing to help us find out who he is? No sign of a weapon?'

'No. We did find something a bit unusual, though.' He held up a transparent evidence bag in his latex gloved fingers. It contained a book, A5 size, with what seemed to be a soft, brown leather cover, very dirty, well thumbed with some pages untidily separated from the binding. Across the cover in faded black type were words in a language I didn't recognise.

Zbierany Poezja 1940 do 1944.

And underneath was written: *Borys Staskiewicz*

Jossie reached for the book then pulled her hand back. We weren't to touch the evidence even if it was in a plastic bag.

'It's Polish. *Collected Poems, 1940 to 1944* by someone called Borys Stasiewicz.'

I'd forgotten that Jossie had Polish ancestry.

'That's all I'll be able to read, though. Most of my Polish has gone.'

Jossie's grandparents came to Australia with many of their countrymen and women after the Second World War. Her parents were born here, so Polish was her second language. She spoke English with a broad Australian accent.

'Anyway,' Farange said, 'we need to get this evidence to the lab.'

'Anything else you can tell us?'

'Flattened grass and footprints close to the pylon where there seems to have been a struggle, then the same two sets of prints leading over to where the body was found. I'm guessing there was a fight, the old bloke tried to get away and the killer followed.'

'The book of poems,' Jossie said. 'Can we have a closer look?'

'Sure. It has to go to the lab, but we'll photograph it for you and send you the printouts.'

'Thanks, Tim, every page please. It might tell us something about him.'

GROUPS of the park's occupants sat in clusters watching and talking. Dog walkers and suited office workers passed by on the path watched by the uniformed police. The morning sun glinted on the river and the first tourist ferry sailed past. A thin crowd of spectators stood along Aquarium Drive. A sunny morning in Melbourne, with all of its lightness and darkness, was underway.

Jossie turned to me, smirking when she said, 'Good luck with the autopsy, Trent. I know how you love them.'

I hated them. *You can't tell me that anyone actually enjoys seeing a human body sliced open and its organs removed, liked some hideous biology experiment, but autopsies are part of the job.* As a team leader, you needed to be there to get a heads-up on the evidence. There was also a weird kind of thing I felt, that I needed to stand guard, to honour the victim as his or her body was being dissected.

'You start on the interviews, Jossie. I'll be back as soon as I can.'

I phoned my boss, Inspector Heather Mattioli, from the car to inform her of the investigation so far. The interviews would take all day, and like most other jobs in a homicide investigation it would be slow, plodding, boring work, but it had to be done. The old bloke deserved at least that.

CHAPTER 15

COLIN BRENNAN

MONDAY, 11 APRIL

Another disaster with Bernadette, and now it seemed that Harry had disappeared.

I was horrified by the fact that Alison had gone home to that situation. Honestly, those two were incapable of being responsible parents. Leo called this morning to tell me that Bernadette was in hospital, and I came right away. They'd taken everything of Alison's out of the house by then, and she was arranging her possessions in Leo's spare bedroom. I was grateful to Leo for the way he'd managed things, making the best decisions he could for Bernadette and Alison.

I'll tell him that soon. I find it hard to give compliments, especially to Leo. There's so much I disapprove of about his lifestyle.

Going to the hospital was pointless. Her doctor refused to allow anyone to see Bernadette yet. Then there was Alison. The two weeks with her at Golden Beach were idyllic, and she relaxed, played, chatted, and laughed, as a young girl should.

Now she was back to this. I had a moment alone with her at the hospital, and she begged me to talk the doctor into allowing her to see her mother. I had to advise against it though, repeating the doctor's recommendation that Bernadette be left alone for a time.

'Think of yourself for a change, dear girl,' I said. 'Your mother's in good hands and is well looked after. She needs time to get better. Concentrate on your own life for a while. Get involved in your school work and sport, and you'll be able to see your mother soon enough.'

I was full of questions, most of which I couldn't admit to anyone.

What is it in Bernadette that makes her unable to deal with life's exigencies? Where is that fool Harry when he's needed? She's my daughter, what is my responsibility here? What should I do to make sure she gets the treatment she needs?

I was an authoritarian father and I knew she was frightened of me. Mary often chided me for it, begging me to be kinder to her. Somehow it wasn't in me. I wasn't patient enough, and my head was always full of a deadline for some complicated judgment. I worked too much, long days in court and in chambers, and I disappeared into my study most weekends.

There were secrets between them, Mary and Bernadette. After the first breakdown, Mary shielded her from everything. She didn't push her when the agoraphobia set in. She allowed her to hide. I didn't agree with it then, but now I was less sure. *My* strategies certainly didn't work.

I would have to stay in Melbourne until everything was sorted out. Alison would be at school, but I'd try to see her in the evenings. I'd booked into the Club, and after an hour or so with Leo, I decided to go back there for lunch. I would go back to the hospital again in the evening, and then I'd take Alison out for dinner.

Leo saw me to the car and stood waiting. There was something he wanted to say. I wasn't good at body language. I should have guessed what was on his mind, but foolishly I gave vent to my own agenda.

'What's wrong with the bloody woman?' I exclaimed in exasperation. 'She's had every possible advantage. Why can't she pull herself together and take care of her daughter? Learned helplessness, that's what it is. And self-pity.'

That was enough to set Leo off. He'd clearly had a very difficult night and day, and he turned on me. 'Dad, this isn't about you. It's about Bernie who, for reasons neither of us understands, needs the support of her family more than anything now. And it's about Alison. Incidentally, it mightn't hurt you to think about your role in this. You've judged and belittled Bernie all her life, even when it was obvious that it was making her worse. She grew up believing that you despised her …'

'Despised?'

'Yes, Dad, despised. I know it's an ugly word, but that's how your attitude came across. Try some empathy for a change, you old bastard. You're not a judge now, and she's not a criminal in your court waiting for you to condescend to sentence her. Think about it. There are all kinds of reasons for Bernie's illness, and just maybe, you're one of them.'

I reeled under the force of his accusations. I slammed the door of the car without saying goodbye and escaped to the privacy of the Club.

In the lounge I sat with a pre-lunch whiskey, and the day's *Australian* spread on the table in front of me. This was usually taken as a sign that you wanted to be left alone, but that convention must have escaped old Rudy Hegarty. He was the garrulous, retired state Liberal backbencher, and all-round political know-all, who was now a fixture of the Club, and its resident motormouth.

'Well, well, Judge Brennan, we don't see much of you these days. Heard you'd locked yourself away in some fishing hamlet on the south coast. Come back to savour the bright lights of the city have you?'

What a bore!

But there was no point in snubbing him. I gave up on the paper and settled in to let him talk. It only needed the occasional nod, or 'Really?' or 'Good God!' or some other neutral exclamation to keep him going.

I did tune in, however, to his stream of irrelevant gossip when he remarked. 'Big funeral at St. Paul's the other day. Surprised you weren't there.'

'Whose funeral?'

'Jack Constable. Didn't you know he'd passed away?'

I didn't know, but doubted I would have gone to his funeral. He and his wife were regular dinner guests at our home in the late eighties. He was a fellow judge, senior to me, and condescending, but the connection was really between Mary and his wife, Sylvia. She was an intimidating, bossy woman whose only personality lay in her organising skills. She'd recruited Mary to some of her causes, and seemed to have decided to take her under her wing.

Although I saw Jack at dinner parties and events for charity that Mary and Sylvia organised, I never liked him. He was a dreary drunk. I loved a whiskey and a good wine, so the drinking itself wasn't the issue, but at a certain point in the evening he would become red-faced, belligerent and argumentative.

Rather than being embarrassed for him, Sylvia would smirk with pride at his boorishness, as if he was a gifted child. I learnt not to interrupt his diatribes against the media, the welfare system, and the latest minority group scapegoat. It was better to nod now and then, and wait for Sylvia to scoop him up to leave. There were rumours about a certain fondness for sleazy table dancing establishments, and once a scandal about an affair with a very young intern in his chambers. Jack was all bluster, and Sylvia publicly dismissed the rumours as just another conspiracy against her brilliant husband.

I was thankful that after Bernadette's breakdown, Mary withdrew from Sylvia's circle of influence, and we didn't have to see the old bore again.

So Jack Constable was dead. I was pleased to have outlived him.

Thankfully, Hegarty left for a lunch appointment elsewhere, and I went alone into the dining room. I asked for a small table by a window, far away from the other lunch guests.

Leo's words replayed over and over in my mind. Had I really despised Bernadette? Could I be one of the causes of her psychiatric illness as Leo had suggested? His words stung — more than stung. I was deeply hurt and angry, but I didn't know who to be angry with. I couldn't blame Leo for his outburst. No, I realised, hardly noticing the food in front of me, that the pain came for a certain unexpressed, half-hidden knowledge of my own that he was right.

I had failed Bernadette — was still failing her.

I felt empty inside, as if I were a brittle glass bowl just waiting for the tap or knock that would shatter it into thousands of pieces. For the first time ever, I felt old and irrelevant.

Mary, I cried silently. *I need you.*

CHAPTER 16
JOSSIE WALLACHIA
MONDAY, 11 APRIL

I GOT TIRED OF PEOPLE TELLING ME I LOOKED TOO YOUNG TO be a detective. I had the track record, six years as a uniformed officer on the streets and then detective school. I'd worked on some big cases that had led to convictions. I was a team player. It was the only way, despite the novels, movies and TV series that glorified the lone maverick.

I had been patronised, hit on, called 'girlie', and subjected to sexist jokes and misogynist banter by colleagues who should have known better. But I didn't take any of it now. They got back what they gave. That was why I loved working with Trent; there was no sub-text. We were professionals, equal colleagues. We worked as a team.

I knew it would be hard to get anything out of the residents of the park. They saw the police as the enemy, there to make their lives more difficult, to move them on, to stop them begging. They'd find it hard to figure me out, a small, blonde woman in jeans, T-shirt and runners claiming to be a Senior Detective.

After the first hour, I gathered my team to compare notes. We had learnt exactly this much: a) The victim was old, crazy, foreign and anti-social; b) No one knew his name; c) He'd been sleeping in the park for about three months; d) Sometimes he raved at passers-by in a foreign language; e) No one had heard or seen anything early that morning when the murder was alleged to have occurred; f) Two people had noticed him sitting by his usual pylon at about midnight, but saw and heard nothing after that.

The next person I interviewed was Stu, a muscular man with a bikie beard. His body was a mosaic of tattoos. He seemed to want to help, but he couldn't tell me much. He did say, though, that I should talk to a woman called Bett, who often slept in the park. He'd seen her talking to the old man once or twice.

'Is she here today?'

'I'll find her for you, love.'

I was writing in my notebook when I looked up and saw a woman coming towards me.

Detectives were trained to register appearance quickly and without surprise, but this time I couldn't help staring. Bett was the last person I expected to find sleeping rough. She seemed to be in her fifties, and she was beautiful, with high cheekbones, widely spaced eyes, dark, thick eyebrows and a generous mouth.

When she smiled at me I saw that, unlike those of many homeless people, her teeth were white and strong. She wore black high-heeled pumps, and the heels sank into the soft grass as she walked. They were real leather, although the caps had fallen off the heels, and the shoes were streaked with mud. I was sure that her soft, slim-fitting jumper was cashmere, although it was dirty and there were food stains across the chest. It was tucked into a light, black wool, knee-length skirt, softly flared. The skirt was crushed, and there were grass and mud stains around the hem. It was beautifully cut.

Casually draped across her shoulders was a red cotton jacket, elegantly made but also grubby. She carried a blue and red silk scarf. Her hair was blonde, long, dry looking, with grey roots that extended from her scalp to just above her ears. It was a long time since she'd had a hairdo.

She stood in front of me, winding the silk scarf around her hair and tying it at the back. Finally she spoke, formally extending her hand. 'Hello, I'm Elizabeth Asher. Pleased to meet you. I understand you're asking about Hobie.' Her voice was educated, cultured, the kind you expected to hear in a mansion south of the Yarra, not in a homeless community under a railway bridge.

'Yes, Ms Asher. I'm Jocelyn Wallachia, a Senior Detective with the Homicide Squad.' I showed her my ID.

'So the deceased was called Hobie?'

She lit a cigarette before she answered. Her dirty fingernails had once been manicured, and they still bore traces of chipped scarlet polish.

'Well that's what he called himself. Listen, dear, I need a cup of tea.'

She was the first person that morning who had shown any personal knowledge of the victim, so a cup of tea was the least I could do. The café in the Aquarium would be open by now.

'Okay, we'll go to the café.'

I spoke to one of my team members briefly, and then I walked with Ms Asher to the café. There would be time for a formal statement later.

'Earl Grey tea, please,' Bett, as she asked me to call her, commanded the hovering waiter while we sat down at a table by the window.

When he came back with her tea, a coffee for myself and a cheese toastie, each on china plates, Bett nodded sniffily. She sat relaxed, her hair now tied up in the silk scarf, and her elegant legs were crossed at the knees. She sipped her tea, nibbled at her sandwich delicately with those expensive teeth, and patted her lips with a napkin.

'So, Hobie?' I began. 'What can you tell me? Was Hobie his real name?'

'I shouldn't think so. No one on the street uses their real name.'

'How well did you know him?'

'Not well, dear. We talked sometimes, usually late at night, especially when his demons began to hound him. He'd sometimes come looking for me then.' Bett paused, for effect I thought. She was enjoying the limelight.

'What demons, Bett?'

'Nazi demons. Hobie was a resistance fighter in Poland under the German occupation during World War II.'

'Can you tell me more about that?'

Even though I had Polish ancestry, I was shamefully ignorant of Poland's war history.

'Well, when the Nazis invaded Poland, the Polish government was exiled to London, but the Home Army, as it was called, fought the invaders. They were an underground group; they fought from hiding, mostly in the forests. Don't you know this history, dear?' she asked accusingly.

I felt like a schoolgirl who hadn't done her homework.

'In Warsaw in 1944, there was an uprising led by that underground Polish army,' she continued. 'The city was destroyed. Hobie was one of 60,000 Poles sent to German camps. He'd already seen terrible things, fellow soldiers murdered in front of him, hundreds of thousands of civilians including children killed in mass executions, and then he witnessed even worse in the camps. No wonder he was a little insane.'

'So he wasn't Jewish?'

'No. Of course it was deadly to be Jewish in Poland then, but Hobie was Catholic, like most Poles. He ended up in a concentration camp. I still can't understand how he survived. Most of the underground military fighters didn't.'

'When did he come to Australia?'

'After the war with all the other displaced people from Poland, and with Jews liberated from the camps.'

'Did he ever mention a family?'

'Once he told me that he had a wife and a son, but then he clammed up and I didn't ask. You learn not to intrude on people's past.'

'What did you talk about with him, Bett?'

'Oh, the evil of human nature. Hobie was a very intelligent man, a philosopher, except when he was able to scrounge money for vodka, then it was best to stay away.'

'What about last night? Did you see or hear anything?'

Bett gave me a defiant stare. She'd tell me what she wanted to tell me when she was ready. 'No dear, I sleep at the other end of the park with my own group. We tend to live in little families here.'

'Was Hobie in a family?'

'No, he was quite antisocial. He hated people.'

'And yet he talked to you?'

'Well, we had something in common, you see.' Bett had finished her tea and sandwich, and she pulled a cigarette and lighter out of the pocket of her jacket.

'You can't smoke in here, Bett. I'll pay the bill and we'll go outside.'

In the warm air she lit her cigarette and blew a white stream out through her nose.

'What did you and Hobie have in common?'

'Hatred of the Nazis and everything German.'

'Are you Jewish?'

'Yes, by blood. You wouldn't exactly call me kosher these days.'

I couldn't ask, not yet, but I wondered again how her life had come down to this, a sleeping bag in a dirty park next to the Yarra.

'My father came out to Australia on the *Dunera,*' she began.

I must have looked blank, because she was suddenly irritated again.

'You young people know no history, do you? It's disgraceful.'

'I'm sorry, Bett, please tell me.'

'Alright, I'll give you a history lesson, little Miss Detective. There were thousands of Jews in England, especially London, just before World War II broke out. They'd fled there when they saw the writing on the wall in Europe. In England, everyone was terrified of a German invasion, and they decided the presence of the Jews would bring on an attack. They put two thousand Jewish boys on a decrepit ship to Australia, the *Dunera*. They spent two months on that stinking overcrowded ship, not knowing where they were going. It docked in Sydney. My father was one of the "*Dunera boys*" as they called themselves, and he made his way to Melbourne in the late 1940s, when members of his family, Holocaust survivors, arrived here.'

'So you were born in Melbourne?'

'Yes, my parents where both Orthodox Jews, so I knew something about Hobie's obsessions. Even as a little girl, I knew the Nazis were monsters. But like many of the *Dunera* boys, my father made the most of his new life and became very successful.'

'Did you have brothers or sisters?'

'No, just me. The full ticket, darling. Exclusive Melbourne Jewish school, synagogue every week, marriage to a brilliant young Jewish investment banker.'

I was amazed. I must have been staring at her, and she didn't like it.

'Grow up, lovey, there's more to the world than your little corner of it,' she barked, dragging on her cigarette. Her long, slim fingers were stained yellow with nicotine.

Clearly I needed to stay out of her personal life.

'Okay, let's get back to Hobie. Did you ever see him talking to anyone else, arguing? Did anyone visit him?'

'No, he was isolate, a recluse. He'd wander during the day and come back to the park at night.'

'Was he concerned for his safety?'

'Another foolish question, darling. Of course he was. We all are, sleeping out in the open like this. He kept his mallet close.'

Mallet? I checked my notes. The crime scene guys hadn't mentioned anything like that.

'He had a mallet?'

Bett was getting tired of this now. 'Yes, he had a mallet,' she mimicked my voice.

I ignored her sarcasm. 'Can you describe it?'

'It was heavy, wooden, a carpenter's mallet. He told me he used to make furniture. He wouldn't let anyone touch it.'

She knew more than she was telling me.

'Bett, I need you to come to the station to make a formal statement. We'll go there now.'

After we left the café, I asked one of the uniformed officers to stay with Bett, while I made arrangements with the rest of my team to continue their investigations in the park.

Then I sent a text to Trent: *Person of interest who knew the deceased. Going now to take a statement. Also possible weapon. How far away are you?*

Trent's reply was almost immediate: *On my way now.*

CHAPTER 17

TRENT GRIERSON

MONDAY, 11 APRIL

BETT WAS ANGRY.

She fiddled with a packet of cigarettes and a lighter, looked around the room, and avoided eye contact.

'What about a cup of tea?' Jossie offered.

That got a response. 'Yes, please.'

When Jossie brought the tea from the kitchen, Bett looked with disdain at the polystyrene cup and its insipid brown liquid.

'Sorry,' Jossie said. 'We don't run to Earl Grey in teapots here.'

'Are we ready to begin?' I asked.

When Bett nodded, I told her of her rights and pressed a button to begin recording the interview.

'You refer to the deceased as Hobie? Do you know his full name?'

Bett seemed now to have decided to cooperate. 'He went by the name Herbert Stanley.'

'Went by? Are you saying it wasn't his real name?'

'Of course not.' Bett couldn't contain her sarcasm. 'It couldn't be. Hobie was Polish. There's nothing Polish about the name Herbert Stanley.'

'How long did you know him?'

'A few years.'

'Did you know him before?' I asked.

Bett seemed to fidget with an invisible cigarette. 'Before? What are you talking about?'

'Before Enterprise Park. Before you became homeless.'

'None of your business.' She crossed her arms defensively.

I was tired. 'Look, Ms Asher, I know this is hard for you. I understand why you don't want to talk to police. But think about it this way. Hobie was your friend. He was violently killed. He was a lonely, homeless old man who didn't deserve that. Don't you owe it to him to help us find the killer? All we want is justice for Hobie. We're not trying to pin anything on you.'

She seemed to relax a little then. 'I met him in 1979. It was the year I was married. He had a furniture factory in Carlton. He made everything himself, heavy European furniture, all Australian hardwood. He was in demand for a few years. We commissioned library shelves for our home in Caulfield, and he came to the house to measure and fit them. He and I talked as he worked.'

'What did you talk about?'

'Literature, history, poetry, social issues, politics, everything. He was an intelligent, well-read man. He told me a little about his life in Poland during the war.'

'Can you remember the name of his factory?'

'Not really ... *Something, Something, Fine Handcrafted Furniture?* I went there a few times. Over the years he made us some beautiful pieces — a table, a dresser, a curved handrail for the main staircase.'

'During what years did you go to the factory?'

Bett thought for a moment. 'Early 1980s.'

'Did anyone work with him?'

'Only the boy that I saw.'

'What boy?'

'Hobie's son.'

'How old was he?'

'Eighteen or so? I didn't know his name. He never spoke.'

'What about the boy's mother?'

'Long gone, Hobie told me.'

'Were you in continuous contact with Hobie since 1979?'

'No, there was a gap of about twenty years when I didn't see him or know where he was. Later he told me that his business failed in the nineties. He survived on the dole and on whatever labour he could get for a few years. By the time I met him again, his alcoholism and "demons" as he called them had taken over and he wasn't able to work.'

'Where was he living then?'

'In a rooming house in Fitzroy.'

'And you?'

'Why does it matter?'

'We have to try to get every piece of information we can. Sometimes something that seems irrelevant turns out to be important.'

Bett rolled her eyes upward in irritation. 'My marriage had finished by then. My husband was in jail for illegal business dealings, embezzlement, insider trading, everything the greedy bastard thought he could get away with. The creditors got everything. I stayed with my parents for a while, and when I couldn't take their disapproval any longer so I started the rounds of emergency housing. It didn't take long to descend into rooming houses, and finally onto the street. Anyway, I met up with Hobie one day at Sacred Heart Mission. All of us down and outs go there for a daily meal. We've stayed together, on and off, since then.'

'So you were a couple?'

'Yes, in a way.' Suddenly her eyes glittered with tears, and she put her head down to hide them.

'Did you know anything about Hobie's son during that time?'

'No, the last time I saw him was at the factory sometime in the early 80s. Hobie didn't know where he was. I've no idea what happened to him.'

'You said that Hobie had a wooden mallet?'

'Yes, it was always close by. He used it in the factory; it was a vintage mallet, very heavy with a long handle.'

'Do you remember him having it when he was living in the park?'

'Yes, as I said. It was always close by. He kept it for protection. When he was drunk he'd wave it at people as if to threaten them, but there was nothing to it. Hobie wasn't violent.'

'This is important. You stated to Detective Wallachia that he had the mallet with him last night, the night he was killed. Are you certain of that?'

'Yes. I was talking to him at about eleven. He was sober and the mallet was there as usual.'

'Anything else you think we should know, Bett?'

'No, I've told you everything.'

'That's all for the time being. If we can't find the son, would you be prepared to identify the body?'

'I suppose so.'

I formally closed the interview and turned off the recorder. 'We'll need to talk to you again. Will we find you at Enterprise Park?'

'Nowhere else to go,' she muttered.

WHILE JOSSIE ORGANISED to have the statement typed up, I stood outside with Bett in the thin autumn sun, as she smoked two cigarettes quickly, drawing the smoke deep into her lungs. I wanted to talk to her about the dangers of sleeping rough, tell her that we could help her find emergency housing, but she was too testy. I tried another approach.

'What about a real cup of tea and a sandwich?' I offered.

I took her to the café next door. It was one of those pretentious, expensive little places where they served five chips in a dented aluminium dish, and sandwiches on a wooden board, but they made real tea in china pots.

'You know, Bett, we could help you get emergency accommodation, and get you on the list for public housing. It's dangerous the way you're living.'

'Look, dear,' she said as she sipped her tea, 'don't worry about me. I've got relatives I could go to, but I can't bear their sanctimonious ways. Every now and then I find emergency housing, but you can never stay very long. They're always moving you on somewhere else. For the time being I'm living in the park. People know me there and look out for me.'

'Well you know you can come to us whenever you're ready, and we'll always do our best to help you.'

Suddenly, uncharacteristically, she reached out her grimy hand and covered mine. It felt almost motherly.

'Thank you, Trent.'

CHAPTER 18

BETT ASHER

MONDAY, 11 APRIL

THOSE TWO WANTED TO RESCUE ME.

God knows, I'd love a bath, love to wash my hair and my clothes, love to feel clean again. But I don't want that more than my freedom. The family suffocates me; all that valiant woman bullshit, the Shabat candles, segregated synagogue, the whole disaster. If I take emergency housing I have public servants wanting to know every detail of my life. I only get the Newstart Allowance, I'm not old enough yet for the pension. On Newstart, I can't afford even the cheapest rent.

Little Miss Detective and that Trent bloke had no idea. How could they understand how two doomed, damaged people could make a home together, even in a cold, wet park? How they could cling together against the rain and wind, how they could calm each other with stories?

Hobie would sing to me the lullabies his mother sang when he was a child. He told me how in Warsaw he saw his wife gunned down, and how part of his heart grew hard and cold that day. He'd told me that he didn't care about his homeland anymore, and then he'd cried and said it wasn't true. He'd recited poetry to me in that language full of hills and valleys, and I'd held him close, dry and warm on our concrete bed.

CHAPTER 19

TRENT GRIERSON

TUESDAY, 12 APRIL

TODAY, THE LAST OF THE AUTUMN WARMTH HAD GONE, AND the sky was that dull, metallic grey, familiar to all of us who lived in this city by the Yarra. I shivered in my hoodie, and Jossie clutched a takeaway coffee in hands covered in fingerless mittens. On the river, two teams on police inflatable boats with outboard motors were setting up dive platforms. One was directly in front of us, only a few metres from Hobie's pylon, and the other was further along, closer to the Aquarium.

We figured that if the murder weapon was indeed Hobie's mallet — and the autopsy had revealed that the injuries to his skull were caused by a heavy, blunt object — the killer wouldn't have wanted to hang on to it. He'd have gotten rid of it quickly, throwing it in the river right away. We were banking on him thinking that there was so much other junk down there that the mallet would never be found.

The inflatable further up the river was just to cover the possibility that the killer threw the mallet in the river as he walked away, towards the Aquarium and King Street.

Sydney people loved to disparage our river, saying that it ran upside down, all the mud on the top. It was murky and brown, and I was glad it was the divers and not me going down there. It was not a deep river, and the experts said it was quite clean, but I wasn't convinced. It was going to be hard for the divers to locate a wooden mallet amid the junk and mud. You couldn't see anything below the surface.

The first team was coming to the surface now. They were empty-handed. I helped to hand them out hot drinks, hoping the second team, now getting ready to go down, would be more successful. We had the divers for the day, but I hoped that if the mallet was there, it would have been found quickly. There was nothing pleasant about this.

The dullness of the river matched my mood on this overcast morning. Alison was like a ghost in our house, silent and traumatised. What a horrible experience, to see your mother forcibly sedated and carried off to a psychiatric clinic. On top of that, her father seemed to have disappeared completely. No one had heard from him, and his phone was dead.

At least, you bastard, I thought, *you could call Alison and let her know that you're okay, find out what's happened to your family.*

Alison kept asking to see her mother, but they said no, as she had to be stabilised.

We'd given our cards to all of the sleepers in the park, asking them to ring us if they thought of anything, however improbable. Most of them had drifted off by now, but Stu, the big, tattooed guy with the bikie beard was hanging around. I wandered over and offered him a cup of coffee from the urn.

'What are they looking for?' he asked.

I was immediately alert. 'Anything and everything. Just seeing what's down there at this stage.'

'Wouldn't be Hobie's mallet, would it?'

I was startled. When he'd spoken to Jossie the previous day, he'd made no mention of knowing the victim's name, or that he owned a mallet.

'How much do you know, Stu?'

He shuffled his big feet in his bikie boots and combed through his grey beard with his fingers. 'Not much.'

'A bit more than you're telling me though.'

He thought about that for a minute. 'No, I knew what he called himself. And you couldn't miss the mallet. When he got pissed he'd threaten people with it.'

'Why didn't you tell Detective Wallachia this?'

'Figured Bett would tell her.' He wouldn't meet my eyes.

'Anything else?'

'I saw him arguing with a bloke a few times. Tall bloke with long hair. Same bloke each time.' He reached into the pocket of his jeans, pulled out a crushed envelope of tobacco, and began rolling a cigarette.

'How many times did you see him? '

'Two, maybe three.'

'What time of day?'

'Around eleven, as people were settling down for the night.' The cigarette was lit and Stu dragged on it hungrily.

'Tell me more about this bloke,' I said, pulling out my notebook and pen.

'As I said, tall. Long, dark hair.'

'Was his hair tied back?'

'No, flopped over his face. Foreign-looking bloke.'

'How old?'

'Hard to say. Fifties?' The tobacco was acrid in the air.

'Could you take a guess at his nationality?'

'A Slav, I'd say, like Hobie. Something about the face. Knew a few of them when I worked in the abattoirs.' The weedy cigarette was finished, and Stu stubbed it into the ground under his boot.

'What did this bloke wear?'

'Old clothes. Trackpants. Nothing you'd remember.'

'Anything else about him?'

'They argued in a foreign lingo.'

'Did you recognise any of it?'

'You've got me there, mate. I don't know one of those European lingos from the next.'

Stu was becoming wary. I couldn't lose him. 'I'm going to need you to come to the station, Stu.'

'Why?'

'Well, you saw someone who may be a suspect. We'll need an artist's impression and a formal statement. Best do it right now.'

I asked Jossie to get one of her team members to take the reluctant Stu back to the station.

'Look after him, Joss,' I said. 'He saw someone who may be a suspect. Get him something to eat if he wants it and make sure we get an artist's impression. And we'll need a detailed statement.'

'Yes, Trent, I know the drill.'

So THE MORNING PASSED, waiting. By two in the afternoon, Jossie was back. Stu's statement and the artist's impression of our suspect were secure back at the precinct. I would study both of them before the day's end. I drifted over to see how the divers were doing, and when I came back, Jossie was on her phone.

'That was my grandfather. I've been thinking about that book of poems that Hobie had. Nothing else, a sleeping bag, a few old clothes, a mallet, no wallet or ID, and this book of poems. It has to be significant. Why would he carry a book of poems when he didn't carry anything else?'

'What's your grandfather got to do with it?'

'He came over after the war. He's very old now, but he still reads and speaks Polish. I thought he might know someone who can tell us more about this poet. I tried on the internet last night, but there was nothing. He says there's someone at Melbourne University who specialises in 20th century Polish literature. I have the name. Should I contact her?'

'Yes, of course, see if we can see her this afternoon or tomorrow. We've got a full copy now, we can show it to her.'

Jossie got on the phone again.

Detective work! You waited around, asked questions, tracked every idea down, followed a lot of loose ends, took the occasional wild goose chase, hoped you'd get lucky, and followed your instincts. But Jossie was right. Homeless people didn't usually carry collections of poems around with them.

'She'll see us this afternoon at four.'

'Good.'

If they hadn't found the mallet by then, it wasn't there.

Suddenly, there was a shout from the divers' platform further along the river near the Aquarium. We ran along the walking path and watched as a diver lifted an object onto the platform. It was a big, primitive hammer, the head consisting of a solid block of dark wood, perhaps eight inches long and three inches respectively broad and deep. The handle was about fifteen inches long, long enough to grip and swing the mallet with some force.

I experienced a moment of elation. This was only the day after Hobie's murder — could we get so lucky? There could even still be fingerprints. We carefully tagged and wrapped it and left it with the divers to deliver to the forensic laboratory, where it would be dried and examined for fingerprints and any traces of DNA.

Back at the station, while Jossie again combed through the interviews from the occupants of the park, I read Stu's statement and examined the drawing of the man he had seen talking to Hobie.

It was only a general impression, and Stu had seen the suspect in the dark, but still, I had to look twice.

Surely not ... it couldn't be!

I quickly dismissed the thought. Lots of men had long, dark hair like that and had those vaguely European features. But at least now we had a possible murder weapon and a suspect, even if we didn't know who he was.

CHAPTER 20

JOSSIE WALLACHIA

TUESDAY, 12 APRIL

'I CAN'T BELIEVE IT! WHAT A RARE AND WONDERFUL FIND. Where on earth did you get it?'

Professor Nadia Godlewski faced us across her desk, in a light-filled office in the Arts building at Melbourne University's Parkville campus.

We'd slipped the photographed pages of Hobie's book of poems into a display folder, and it was these that she now examined.

'Where's the original book?' she asked. 'I hope it's somewhere safe.'

She was imposing, a large, attractive woman, not young, with a long mane of curly dark hair that fell around her shoulders, and clear, white skin devoid of make-up. She wore a maxi dress of red cotton in a batik design, and a necklace of heavy, black beads. She spoke with a slight accent.

'It's evidence in an ongoing investigation, which we can't say too much about,' Trent explained. 'It's being held securely until the investigation's over. What you have there is a full copy. When you say rare, Professor …?'

'It's Nadia. Oh, very rare. There were only about thirty of these printed. I didn't know there were any in Australia. Borys

Stasiewicz was a hero of the anti-Nazi Resistance in Poland. He was a soldier of the Home Army, and one of the leaders of the Generation of Columbus, as they called themselves.'

'Why Columbus?' Trent queried.

'The generation born in Poland after 1918. They saw themselves as discoverers of a new Poland, hence Columbus. The term was usually used for the young intelligentsia like Stasiewicz, but it applied to the whole generation. Most of them were Resistance fighters in some way.'

I listened intently. My grandfather was born in Poland in the 1920s. We had never spoken of his experiences.

Nadia continued, 'The young generation of Polish poets was at the centre of the Resistance. Just as they fought the Nazis in the forests and alleyways, they also fought in words using their poetry. Most of them were killed in the Warsaw uprising in 1944.'

'Tell us about Borys Stasiewicz?' I prompted.

'He was brilliant. Although he was very young, he lectured in Polish language at the Warsaw University. When the university went underground during the German and Soviet occupations, he continued to teach, all the while writing his poetry. In 1943, he joined the Home Army. He was a very active soldier, keeping an arsenal of weapons in his apartment and taking part in several sabotage actions. He and his wife, Maria, distributed nationalistic literature and poetry from their apartment. It was Maria who ensured his poems were collected and printed. She was pregnant with their first child when she was killed in the 1944 uprising. Stasiewicz saw her shot down and risked his own life holding her in his arms as she died.'

There was little we could say in the face of such horror. Nadia continued leafing through the folder as if it was a precious sacred text.

'Neither of us are Polish speakers, so we haven't been able to read the poems. What kind of poetry is it?' Trent asked.

'Anti-war, full of nationalistic passion. He was a devout

Catholic, so there's a lot of very rich religious symbolism and imagery. He was a hero among his contemporaries, not just for his courage in resisting oppression, but also for his inspirational poetry. Despite the rivers of blood he must have seen, whole families cut to pieces, the cruellest imaginable crimes of war, his poetry is full of a longing for peace.' She paused, reverently turning the pages. 'Oh Lord, I'd love to show these poems to my students.'

Trent took up the questioning again. 'What happened to Stasiewicz? Did he survive the war?'

'We don't know. There's no record of him dying in the Warsaw uprising, but that doesn't mean much. It was a blood bath and many bodies were never recovered. It's possible that he ended up in one of the German camps in Poland. There were hundreds of them across the country, and it wasn't just Jews who were sent to them. They were filled with Poles and Checzs. The majority died from starvation, disease and forced labour in terrible conditions, when they were literally skin and bone, as well as regular mass executions. There's also no record of Stasiewicz dying in the camps, but the Nazis didn't worry too much about preserving the identity of prisoners who were destined for mass graves anyway. There's also no record of him entering any country that took Polish refugees after the war, so it's all a mystery.'

'So we don't know if he died in the war or outlived it.'

'No, we don't. But the person who owns this book knew Borys Stasiewicz. The copies were distributed around a very tight circle. It's an incredible find.'

'Could he have survived the camps and changed his name?'

'It's possible. He may have just taken on the identity of one of his dead confreres, or he may have made up a completely new identity. That would have been quite easy. Many of them arrived in Australia with no identity papers at all.'

'Why would he need to change his identity?'

'Paranoia; fear of the long reach of the Nazi arm; the desire to forget the past.'

'There's no information about him on the internet,' I volunteered.

'Yes there is, but you need to go into the Polish language sites. Give me a minute or so and I'll see what I can find.'

Nadia tapped on her keyboard while we waited.

'Ah, here, a full chronology of his life, copies of his poems, all in Polish I'm afraid.'

'Is there a photo?'

'Yes.'

She turned her computer around so we could see the screen. A young man, no more than twenty-two or three looked out at us. He had an open, intelligent face, dark hair and eyes. It was an idealistic face, full of hope — the kind of face that still believed, despite all the opposing evidence, that justice was possible.

I looked at Trent. I knew he had the same question I had.

'Nadia, could you send that site to the technical officer at our station, please?'

'Of course.'

I gave her the address, and while she sent it I thought of my grandfather. Would he have known of Borys Stasiewicz? Perhaps at the weekend I'd pay him a long overdue visit and ask him.

'Thank you, Nadia, your help has been invaluable,' I said, handing her my card, along with Trent's. 'Please call immediately if you think of anything else that may be of interest.'

'What's of interest to me is the book from which these pages were photographed. It's priceless.'

'Priceless?'

'Not in monetary terms, but as part of the history of Poland and its literature. You can't put a value on it. I hope you'll take good care of it, and when your investigation is over, perhaps you can donate it to an institution that will understand its importance and keep it safe where people can have access to it.'

There was very little we could promise at this stage, but we thanked her again and almost ran to the car.

BACK AT THE STATION, we were just in time to catch the computer tech before he left for the afternoon.

'Trev, there's an email for you with an image we need you to look at. I know you want to go home, but we wouldn't ask if it wasn't urgent.'

Trevor sighed, took off his jacket, and sat in front of his computer. Stasiewicz's young face came onto the screen.

'Can you age the image? Show us what this face would look like after seventy or so years?'

'Okay.'

We waited — tense.

It took less than a minute for Hobie's face to emerge from the features of the young poet.

Hobie, our murdered homeless man, who went by the name of Herbert Stanley, was Borys Stasiewicz, poet and resistance fighter, hero of the Polish underground and passionate Polish nationalist.

'Found you, Borys,' Trent said. 'Now let's find out who killed you.'

CHAPTER 21

TRENT GRIERSON

WEDNESDAY, 13 APRIL

WE'D STARTED COMBING THROUGH THE YELLOW PAGES FROM 1979, looking for handcrafted furniture businesses in Carlton. There were a dozen or so. We phoned them all, and deleted any that were still operating. That left us with eight. We got an assistant to go through back records to find information about their owners, but it was thirty-seven years ago. We weren't hopeful.

Just when I was beginning to think we'd hit another road-block, a courier delivered the forensic report on Hobie's mallet. Two sets of prints had been found, one set was Hobie's, identified from the autopsy, and the other belonged to someone called Henryk Stanley.

Our luck was improving.

Henryk Stanley had been brought in for minor offences years before, and his prints were still in the system. It only took minutes to find his mug shot and bring it up on the screen. He had been twenty-five years younger, but there was no mistaking him — the big head and face, the hunched shoulders, the long, dark hair parted in the middle and reaching his collar, the bull like neck and chest.

It was a moment in my policing career that I would never forget.

Henryk Stanley was Harry, Alison's father.

CHAPTER 22
ALISON BRENNAN
THURSDAY, 14 APRIL

SELMA FERGUSON WAS THE UNDISPUTED PRINCESS OF OUR YEAR level.

She had long, blonde hair and perfect skin, and she cultivated that pouty, vacant expression you saw on models in magazines. Everyone knew that she had parts in *Home and Away* and that she had a contract with a modelling agency. She was the centre of an eager group of girls who radiated around her in dread of being the next one to be dropped or humiliated on social media. To Selma, I must have been worse that invisible, like a boring, grey stone. I didn't vie for her attention, and I didn't gossip.

But Rosa Spinella became Selma's latest target. Rosa was new, so I didn't know her well. She wasn't in one of the friendship cliques yet, and I was a well-known loner, so we sometimes gravitated together.

On Monday, Rosa and I were at the lockers getting ready for the day. Rosa was sipping from a takeaway cup of coffee. Suddenly, as she reached into the back of her locker for her diary, Selma walked past and lurched against her, upending the coffee down the front of Rosa's dress.

'Sorr … eee,' Selma said, and then she walked off with her coterie of giggling subordinates.

'That was deliberate,' I said, staring after them.

'I know, she does it all the time,' Rosa said, dabbing at her dress with tissues.

'Come on, we've got time. I'll help you wash it off in the bathroom.'

It was quiet there, and we did the best we could to clean the stain.

'What do you mean "all the time"?' I asked.

'Bitchy comments about my appearance, my name … supposed to be private but loud enough for me to overhear.'

'Your name? Rosa? What's that about?'

'Spinella. It's Italian.'

'And?'

'How many other girls with Italian names are there at this school? They're like "Go back to your fruit and vegetable stall".'

'Rosa, that's bullying.'

'I know.'

'Tell someone.' I urged.

'Really? Sure. That should help.' We both knew it would be pointless.

TODAY in our English Literature class, Rosa and I sat together near the front of the room. Rosa wasn't like me. I was every teacher's dream student. I was quiet. I did my homework, and I never disrupted the class, but Rosa was funny and a bit weird. She doodled strange little faces in her diary, mimicked the teachers behind their backs, and she always asked questions no one else thought of, especially in Mr Jordan's class.

Mr Jordan, our English Literature teacher, was the youngest teacher in the school, and the nerdiest. He combed his dark hair back off his forehead, and he seemed to use that old-fashioned hair oil that you sometimes saw in vintage advertisements. Every day he wore a white shirt with a bow tie, and over the shirt he wore a cardigan. Yes, an actual cardigan.

He always matched his bow tie to one of the colours in his cardigan. He wore shiny, brown, lace-up schoolboy shoes with white socks. He had black-framed glasses with thick lenses, and he had a habit of pulling down the right sleeve of his cardigan to polish his glasses on the cuff. He did this as he stared into space, or out the window, or while he was listening to someone read or explain something about one of our texts.

As geeky as he was, I had a major crush on him. It wasn't his looks or what he wore, or even that he was patient and quiet, not like some of the other teachers whose mouths were as big as their egos. No, it was his voice. When Mr Jordan recited a poem (he seemed to know by heart every poem that had ever been written), the words flooded over me like deep, rich music. He recited poetry as if he was in love with its beauty, as if he marvelled at it. His awe for a poem was so strong — you couldn't help but feel that same awe too.

I got caught up in the words too, and I wanted to listen to him all day. He said that the best way to appreciate poetry was to read it aloud to yourself, and so I did, when I was alone at night, listening to the cadences as they danced off my tongue.

But it was not only poetry. Mr Jordan said that the stories in our set novels were not just single stories, but hundreds of stories. They were stories about everyone everywhere, stories about us. I saw deeper into the novels now, looking for the bigger stories. Mr Jordan was the best teacher I'd ever had.

This term we were studying Sonya Hartnett's novel, *Surrender.* Mr Jordan asked us to read a chapter a night, and to keep a journal of our reactions as we read it. We were to write 500 words in response to each chapter. We had to handwrite it, in a proper lined exercise book. He said (not knowing why) that in handwriting, you could pour more of your soul onto the page. We were to keep the exercise book with us at all times. It was our writer's notebook, as well as the journal where we recorded our reactions to the texts.

Every day Mr Jordan asked five different students to read from their journal. Usually he didn't set a topic, he liked us to give unedited reactions to what we'd read, but yesterday he gave us the theme of 'identity' as an introduction to one of the big themes of the novel.

'What is identity?' he asked. 'Where does it come from, what influences it, does it change over time?' He threw questions at us, but he wouldn't give us a prescriptive list. He said that we must chase the questions down as a child chases a balloon, and if a different question or idea catches our interest, we must chase that one instead.

In class today, he asked Rosa to read her excerpt on identity. I knew she hadn't done it, but she sat with her notebook in front of her face and gave an amazing discussion of the theme. She explained how identity was shaped by home, school, family and wider society, how it could be damaged by trauma, how people our age liked to try on different identities, how identities could sometime split off under pressure into multiple identities, until finally 'when you're old', she said, identity settled down into something comfortable.

She didn't falter once. It was fluent, thoughtful, reflective and clever, but she was reading from a blank page. I knew that because I was sitting next to her, but no one else knew.

Except Mr Jordan.

'Wonderful, Rosa,' he said, polishing his glasses on his sleeve and staring out the window as if an irresistible spectacle was taking place out there, one that only he could see. 'Please bring the written version to me at the beginning of tomorrow's class, as well as tonight's entry.'

Was there a tiny, almost uncontrollable smile on his face as he turned back towards the class?

'You're crazy,' I said to Rosa as we packed up our books.

'I know, but isn't he sweet? What are you doing for lunch?'

'Nothing. I'm going to the library to borrow some books.'

'Library? At lunchtime? How boring. Come with me to watch the netball. The Year Eleven team's playing Melbourne Grammar in the gym.'

So we sat in the stands with salad rolls from the canteen and watched the teams expertly handle the ball from one end of the court to the other. I'd never played netball, and I was amazed how fast the game was. You couldn't stop watching for a second or you'd miss a spectacular pass or a goal. The girls ran, jumped, guarded their opponents, threw goals and called encouragement to each other, and just briefly, I forgot Sunday night's horrible scene when the ambulance took Mum away, and the anxiety I felt for her like a stone in my guts.

As we wandered back towards the classrooms, Rosa asked, 'Do you want to hang out at the weekend?'

Immediately I was tense. My stomach clenched. I couldn't tell her the truth. 'Oh, my mum's in a mental hospital, my dad's disappeared, our house is a tip and I'm temporarily staying at my uncle's place.'

So I lied. 'It's hard at my house. Mum's sick and you can't make any noise.' It was as good a story as any.

'Oh, I'm sorry. What's wrong with her?'

I embellished quickly. 'She gets terrible migraines. They go for days.'

'How awful. Well, come to my place. We can make as much noise as we like there. My older brother works on Saturdays, and Gio plays soccer, so we'll have the house to ourselves. We can binge on movies.'

I wanted to say yes, but Rosa's friendship would come at a cost to me. I would have to keep my home and family secret, and it was exhausting. She'd start to wonder why I never brought her home. *Migraines don't last that long, do they?*

At an earlier time, I would have turned away, but something was uncoiling in me now, because of Mrs Goodall, and

Golden Beach, and my beautiful rosewood desk. Rosa's offer of friendship was like a tantalising vision bobbing ahead of me, just out of reach. I only had to stretch out, catch hold of it, try it on as you try on a new top, and if it wasn't right I could give it back. Or so I told myself anyway.

'Sounds good. So how old's Gio?'

'Only eight. He's totally gorgeous. Sometimes, just sometimes, that compensates for the loud, boorish brother, Dario, or Deegs, as his moron mates call him.'

'Does he work full time?'

'No, he's at uni. He works in a music store at the weekends. He has a sixties music fetish. He knows everything about everything. Really, it's best to ignore him.'

'Dario? Gio? Is that Giovanni? Do you speak Italian?'

'My parents were born here, but that doesn't stop them making us talk Italian at home whenever the mood takes them. So what about Saturday?'

'Yes, I'd love to come, but I warn you, I'm quiet and boring. Can I bring some DVDs?

'What have I done?' I badgered myself as I hurried to my Maths class. Is it too late to get out of it? I could say I had to work, that Hungry Jacks had called me in for an extra shift. I could say that Mum needed me; I could say that I was sick; I could say that I had an urgent assignment.

Then I tried to imagine how Mrs Goodall would respond …

'Relax, Alison, all you've done is agree to spend a few hours on Saturday with a girl from school. No commitment, no return visits — and let's face it, you need a friend.' Then she'd say in her calm, objective voice … *'You're doing very well, Alison.'*

CHAPTER 23
ALISON BRENNAN
SATURDAY, 16 APRIL

ROSA LIVED IN NORTHCOTE, IN A DOUBLE-STOREY RED BRICK house. It had two white iron balconies facing the street on the upper level, and a wider white balcony on the lower level. They made the house look friendly, as if the upstairs balconies were the house's eyes and the lower balcony a smile.

I was nervous. I couldn't say anything as Rosa showed me around. I hoped I wasn't gawking. It was the kind of house I imagined for myself in the long night hours as I listened to the rats scurrying outside my bedroom. It wasn't just the sparkling white tiles and honey-coloured wooden cabinets in the kitchen, or even the bare, pale wooden floors of the family room with its minimal furniture, and wood fire. It wasn't the thick ivory carpets of the bedrooms upstairs, or the same honey glowing wood of the cabinets in the bathrooms.

No, what I loved was that it was all so uncluttered, almost spartan. There was nothing that wasn't necessary, just a few prints breaking up the white walls, and one panel in the family room covered in photos of Rosa, her parents and brothers, and other people I guessed were her extended family.

The house was very clean and neat — the only thing on the kitchen bench was a wire basket full of fruit — but it wasn't sterile or cold. It felt like a happy house, and you could tell a family lived there. There was a wooden deck leading from the family room, and on it was a big basket of logs waiting for the fire. There was a gas barbecue there, as well as a soccer ball, a football and a cricket bat. There were bikes in the garage next to the deck, and skateboards and skis.

Rosa told me that her mother was a seamstress. One of the rooms on the top floor was her workroom, and it contained her sewing machine, an ironing board and a cabinet that took up a whole wall. The shelves of the cabinet were fitted with little drawers, there must have been fifty of them. Rosa opened some to show me. Every colour of thread you could imagine was in one drawer, hundreds of buttons of different shapes and colours in another, sequins in another, tiny pearls, laces and ribbons, and a life-sized mannequin. There was everything you would need to make gorgeous clothes. The windows, which were covered in a soft, drapey, transparent fabric, framed a view of the city.

'We're not allowed in here,' Rosa said. 'It's Mum's room. Sometimes if I need to talk to her and she's busy, she'll let me come in, and we talk as she works, but not often.'

I coveted that room. I wanted its couch with the bright cushions, its windows with their gauzy curtains, its spotless carpet without a single thread or piece of fabric spoiling its perfection. I wanted it even more than I wanted Rosa's room, which was as bright and clean as the rest of the house and decorated with larger versions in charcoal of the quirky caricatures she drew in her diary.

You just knew that the people who lived in this house loved it and were proud of it.

That settles it, I said to myself. *Rosa will never, ever see my house.*

I thought about houses a lot. I knew I was going on about Rosa's place, but I hadn't been in many houses. There was Uncle Leo's, of course, and Grandpa's, and Lo-an's, my friend from primary school. Sometimes there was a party at another girl's house for the swimming team, but that was it. Mum and Dad never went anywhere. They'd never even taken me to other people's houses.

It was fun being with Rosa. We talked about school and the teachers with their funny or weird habits. Rosa mimicked our homeroom teacher's strong American accent so perfectly that I rolled on the couch laughing. We talked about assignments and what we wanted to do when we left school. We made sandwiches and iced coffee and watched two episodes of *Breaking Bad* on Netflix. Rosa waxed my eyebrows and I tried on some of her makeup. I didn't say anything about Mum being in hospital or Dad's disappearance. How could I?

Late in the afternoon, Rosa's mother and little brother came home.

Mrs Spinella was an older version of Rosa. She had the same neat, black hair that seemed to fit over her head like a close cap. She wore big, gold hoops in her ears, and bright red lipstick. She was small — elfin was the word I thought of — and she was dressed all in black: black leggings, a black jumper, which came almost to her knees, and black ankle boots. I wondered if she made her own clothes.

'Leave your runners outside, Gio,' she called. 'Well, what have you girls been doing?'

'You know, mucking around,' Rosa answered vaguely. 'Talking, watching stuff.'

Gio looked to be in about Year Three. He was a curly-haired little boy, dark, with olive skin and brown eyes. He cuddled up to Rosa on the couch, and she put her arms around him.

'Did you kill them at soccer today, my hero?' she asked.

'Nah, not today. We lost.'

'Next week then.' Rosa kissed him on the top of his head.

I didn't know it was like that, having a little brother.

'Come any time, Alison,' Mrs Spinella said as I left.

'Do you want to meet Dad before you go?' Rosa asked as

we left by the front door. When I nodded, she led me to the tram stop on the other side of High Street, in the opposite direction from where I would get the tram home.

'He has a food truck,' she said, as we left the tram two stops down the busy street. We walked into a big open area ringed with trucks selling all kinds of food, Mexican, Chinese, Vietnamese, Indian, Spanish, hamburgers and ice cream. Rosa's dad's truck was called 'Pasta Face', and in front of its open serving window there was a long queue of people.

Mr Spinella sold pasta and pizza, lots of different varieties, but also other Italian dishes such as meatballs in tomato sauce, handmade Italian sausages, chicken, beef and vegetarian pasta sauces. There was a cabinet full of delicious-looking desserts.

When we got to the top of the queue, Rosa introduced me. 'Dad, this is my friend Alison.' And then to me, proudly, she said, 'Dad makes everything himself. He's a chef.'

I thought of cooking in that spotless kitchen at Rosa's house, how satisfying it would be.

Mr Spinella was big and loud. He was delighted that we had visited him. He called to another man who was working with him in the truck. 'Look, Stevo, Rosa's here with her friend. What do you girls want to eat? We've got a special seafood pasta today. It's walking out the door. Take some, Alison.' He scooped an enormous portion into a plastic container, snapped on the lid, and pushed it at me. 'Here, darling.'

The pasta smelled heavenly, but there was much more than I could eat. I'd share it with Trent and Leo.

'Come back and help me Rosa when you've said good bye to your friend,' he called as we walked away.

'What will you do?' I asked.

'Oh, serve the customers, collect money, clean, whatever Dad needs me to do.'

'Do you help every weekend?'

'No, only if he asks me. He used to have a restaurant when we lived in Sydney, and I worked there at the weekends, but he sold that and bought the food truck when we came here. He's much happier now, and he's home much more. Because he's happier, everyone's happier. The food truck is open mostly at the weekends, but during the week, only in the evenings. He can take Gio to school, help Mum in the house. He was always worried about the business when we lived in Sydney.'

Now I knew a lot about Rosa's family, but she hadn't asked any questions about mine. I wondered what she thought. What would I tell her if she asked?

Rosa walked with me to my tram stop. 'See you on Monday,' she said, hugging me.

I hugged her back.

That's what normal's like, I thought as I found a seat on the tram. *Normal family, normal house, normal friendship.*

'Well, Alison,' Mrs Goodall's voice sounded in my head. *'What was so hard about that? Admit it, you enjoyed it. Rosa's nice.'*

'But the secrets I'll have to keep,' I answered silently.

'Every family's got secrets, Alison. Anyway, give people credit. Sometimes they're more accepting and understanding that you expect them to be.'

CHAPTER 24
HARRY (HENRYK STANLEY)
SATURDAY, 16 APRIL

THEY'LL COME FOR ME SOON. I'M READY. I KNOW WHAT I'M going to do.

I'd gone back to the house. Bernie and Alison had gone, and I didn't know where they were. I could find out, but there was no point now. I wasn't going to be around long enough.

Sitting in the kitchen, I waited. I would know when they were there.

In the end, Bernie and I didn't make much of a go of it. The only good thing was Alison. When she was born, I thought I'd start again. I gave up the grog. I was wild and stupid before that, getting hauled into the cop shop for fighting, being drunk and disorderly — you name it.

I was never much of a provider. We lived on Bernie's money, and the old Judge owned the house. Sure, I could mend things, lift things, I was strong, but I never learnt to make furniture like the old man. I was a disappointment. A different kind of son might have saved him, given him something to hope for. Not me.

I remembered being at school for a while, trying to learn to read, but I couldn't get it. Got just enough now to get my licence and put my bets on. We moved around too much anyway. Always some camp in the bush with other 'dagos', as they called us, logging, building dams, always freezing and wet.

Dad picked up a Polish woman in one of the camps. That's where I was born. She left when I was a baby. I had a sort of dim memory of her bending over a cot, saying something in Polish. Touching my cheek. Then she was gone, the hut empty. From there it was just the old man and me.

He used to belt me, especially when he was drunk. I was always scared when he went to the tavern. I use to pretend to be asleep when he got home, but he would drag me from bed, yelling about something I'd done or hadn't done. He was crazy. He'd scream at me in Polish. 'Is this what I lived through the war for? To be stuck with a retarded kid.' Then he'd hit me across the skull, and my head would start with the ringing noise. The only thing I could do was run out into the cold and hide until he sobered up.

It was better when we came to Melbourne and had the furniture business. He was making money, and customers respected him. We lived well then, and he didn't get angry so often. Anyway, I wasn't scared of him anymore. I was bigger and stronger than him. He got drunk less, but when he did, he just sat in a corner with his old book of poems and read it softly to himself. I knew he wrote the poems in Poland during the war, but that was all I knew.

I left when the business went broke. I took labouring jobs, and when I got some money together I bought a truck and a lawnmower and went gardening. That was when the Judge took me on for that big garden of his, and I met Bernie and I felt sorry for her. I took her away. She didn't need much persuading. Bernie needed someone to help her, but in the end I wasn't up to it. She needed more than I could give her.

Not Allie though. She was something special. She was beautiful and smart, and she deserved better than the mess

Bernie and me made. I had decided to get out of her life now, to give her a chance.

The stupid thing was that I didn't go there to kill the old boy. Just like the other times — I just wanted to make sure he was okay. I'd known for a few months that he was living rough, and I wanted to help him. But he picked a fight, told me to piss off, that he didn't need me. That night it was worse. He was raving, but the funny thing was he wasn't drunk. But the abuse!

It was my fault my mother had left, my fault I was a retard, my fault he was stuck here and hadn't been able to go back to Poland. He started swinging that bloody mallet, and I didn't know, all the years of beltings came back, and I was hot, hot, angry, saw red in front of my eyes. I wanted to kill him there and then. I grabbed the mallet and swung it once, twice, three or four times. His head smashed like a pumpkin.

Then I realised what I'd done. I was pretty sure no one had seen me. It was early hours, well after midnight. I didn't know what to do, so I ran. I dumped the mallet in the river. Never went home. I had been sleeping rough like the old boy.

But now it was time. So there I was, and I was ready.

I'd cleared a path to the front door and I was standing there waiting.

First to appear was a big bloke in a suit, a small, blonde woman, and three police in uniforms.

They didn't need all those coppers, I thought. I was going to go with them. They would get a confession. I wasn't scared of jail.

But there was one thing I had to do first …

I'd already soaked the piles of paper and rubbish in petrol, and before I went out to meet them, hands in the air, I threw a match. I heard and smelt it, just a crackling at first, then windows smashing, flames bursting through the roof, coppers yelling, somewhere there was a fire engine.

My lovely Allie, this house will never be a problem for you again.

CHAPTER 25
TRENT GRIERSON
SATURDAY, 16 APRIL

WHEN WE REALISED THAT THE SUSPECT WAS HARRY, I WAS obliged to remove myself from the investigation. Jossie and I briefed Senior Sergeant Frank McLeod, and I had to leave the arrest to him. But something made me follow them at a distance, and I sat in my car on the other side of the road a little away from the house.

When Harry emerged, the house exploded behind him. One second he was walking towards Frank, hands in the air, and the next thing flames were shooting through the shattered windows, and leaping and crackling through the rubbish piled at the door.

From where I stood, every part of the house was on fire. Inside it would have been an inferno. Frank and the uniformed officers ran to Harry and pulled him to safety, as Jossie and the other cops ran to evacuate the houses on either side.

'Anyone else inside, Harry?' Frank yelled.

'Nah, only me.'

From where I stood he looked quiet, relaxed, staring at the house, fascinated. Someone had rung for fire engines, and I could hear their high-pitched squeal a block away. Families from the houses alongside stood apart, holding children and animals. Spectators were gathering and the police were putting up barriers.

Another two uniforms had arrived and were standing with Harry, who was now handcuffed. In the midst of it all, everyone accounted for, everyone safe, the fireys doing their job, the uniformed officers on guard, I had a moment of clarity.

Burn down … keep on burning till nothing is left.

You had to be steely in this job. Empathy was not your friend; facts were all that mattered. So I had to fight back the memory of Harry putting a heavy lock on Alison's bedroom door to protect her precious desk, her only link to her grandmother; the memory of Harry helping me to throw junk into the skip the day after we cleared Alison's room; and the impression he left with me of a man caught between two nightmares.

Perhaps the flames could bring to ash some of the unhappiness that had lived in that house.

When the house was just a smouldering shell, they took Harry in.

CHAPTER 26

JOSSIE WALLACHIA

SATURDAY, 16 APRIL

I DROVE WHILE FRANK SAT IN THE FRONT PASSENGER SEAT, AND one of the uniformed coppers sat with Harry in the back. He was as quiet and calm as a sleepy cat.

Back at the station we read him his rights but we weren't recording anything yet. Just having a chat.

Harry had been thinking though. 'Look mate,' he said to Frank. 'I don't want to make this hard for you, but shouldn't I have a lawyer?'

'Is there a particular one you want?'

'Don't know any.'

'Okay, we'll go through Legal Aid.'

We took him to a cell to wait. Even though it was Saturday morning, the solicitor arrived an hour later. It was Tom McCauley, an affable man in his early seventies, a veteran of the criminal court and well known in police and legal circles.

Frank and I met with McCauley first and outlined our case against Harry. We weren't charging him yet, just gathering information. We had his fingerprints on the murder weapon and eyewitness reports of someone fitting his description arguing with the deceased.

It was quicker than any of us expected. Old McCauley

spent half an hour in the cell with Harry then he was brought to the interview room. Frank reminded him of his rights and started the video recorder, first checking his name, address and birth date.

'What do you know about the death of Borys Stasiewicz?'

Harry obviously wanted to tell the story, so he got straight into it. 'I don't want to string this out. The old man was my father. I didn't go there to kill him, but that's what happened. Right?'

'You don't have the same surname?'

'Stanley was the surname he gave me when I was born. He used it for himself mostly too. Said he didn't want to remember that he was Polish.'

The solicitor was silent as Harry spoke. They'd obviously agreed to this confession, hoping for a lesser charge and a shorter sentence.

We Anglo-Australians, I thought, *have been so protected. Few of us have known dispossession, murder in the streets, mass executions, colleagues and loved ones mowed down before our eyes, and the psychological desert that must follow.*

Harry's limited vocabulary, his inability to make anything more than verbal line drawings of Borys's experiences, made the story stark, unreal. But Borys's past had become Harry's own, drilled into him over years of his father's drunken soliloquies.

The story limped along — the lonely, rainy nights in forest camps, his mother's desertion, the inevitability of mental and physical abuse, the knowledge that his father saw him as an embarrassment, the factory in Carlton, Harry now a tall, heavy man, no longer afraid of Borys's violence.

'Lost track for years, then went looking for him one day at that rooming house in St Kilda. One of the old boys there told me Hobie, as he called himself, was sleeping rough. He said to try that park on the river, down from Flinders Street.'

He found him there a few times, wanted to help. He

offered to find him somewhere to live, but the result was always the same, incoherent drunken abuse or worse, the familiar sarcasm and insults.

Late on that Sunday night, he went there once more. It was to be the last time.

'I was going to leave him to rot after that,' Harry recalled.

We knew the rest. The mallet was there. The killing was impulsive and brutal. Realising what he had done, Harry panicked, threw the mallet in the river and ran. He hid in parks around the city until he knew, from pieces of overheard news bulletins, that a murder weapon had been found.

Then he had gone home to wait. No one was there. Bernadette's impression was still in the empty bed, but his daughter's room had been cleared of all her possessions. He seemed to accept their disappearance as inevitable. He didn't believe anyone would value him enough to stay around.

THE LAWYER NEGOTIATED the lesser charge of manslaughter in return for a guilty plea. Harry didn't want bail.

'Nowhere to go, mate,' was his only comment.

We arranged his transfer to the Melbourne Assessment Centre, where he would receive a psychiatric assessment and await a trial date. The next day, news of the charges would be in the Sunday papers and heading news bulletins. His family should be told before that.

'Is there a family member you want to talk to at this stage, Harry?' Frank asked.

'Is Trent about? Don't know his surname. He's a homicide cop too.'

We knew Trent was in the building, so we called him in. He was no longer on the investigation, but Frank gave him permission to stand in as a family member.

'Where are Bernie and Allie, Trent?' Harry asked.

He explained briefly what had happened on the previous

Sunday — Bernie's hospitalisation and Alison's move to her uncle's home. 'She's safe, Harry,' he assured him.

'Tell her before it's on the news.'

'Of course.'

There was something else he wanted to say. He hesitated for a moment, made to go, and then he turned back. 'Tell her I'm sorry; tell her I love her.' Then his voice strained. 'Tell her I'm no good; she should forget me.'

The big face was twisted in grief. It was the only emotion he'd shown. No regret for his father's death, no concern for Bernie, only remorse, guilt, words of love for Alison.

CHAPTER 27

LEO BRENNAN

SATURDAY, 16 APRIL

I WAS PHOTOGRAPHING A BRIDAL PARTY IN THE BOTANIC Gardens in that soft autumn sun you get in Melbourne, when Trent's call came. I asked the bride and groom to take a break so I could return the call. Trent never rang unless it was urgent.

'I can't give you the details now, but I need to talk to you about something important before you see tonight's news. After that you'll need to talk to the Judge.'

It took me a second to register what he was saying. 'What's this about, Trent?'

He seemed breathless, tense. His voice was urgent. 'Can't answer questions now. It's going to be all over the media. When will you be finished? Ring the Judge. You're going to need to see him tonight.'

'What's the big secret?'

'Please, Leo, just do what I'm asking. I'll explain everything later. I have to go. '

I hated mysteries, but Trent wasn't going to tell me anymore, and besides, I had work to do. We agreed to meet at home at four o'clock. I phoned the Judge and invited myself to dinner at the Club, recalling that he was planning to return to Golden Beach tomorrow. I was a little ashamed of my attack on him last Monday, but we'd spoken since then and neither of us had mentioned it.

Along with whatever Trent's secret was, tonight might be the opportunity for me to apologise, and perhaps to break down some of the wall between us. Alison was at her friend's house and I was expecting her back for dinner, but I hoped Trent could be there with her.

I WAS home by four and Trent was waiting, his face full of something I couldn't decipher.

'We'd better sit down.'

So I sat; I was scared now. 'What is it, Trent?'

'It's Harry! There's no easy way to tell you. He's been charged with killing that homeless man in Enterprise Park.'

'Harry?'

'Yes, Harry, Alison's dad.'

My mind was woolly. *Harry? Alison's dad? Killing? Homeless man?* None of it connected.

'Leo. Just listen. Let me take you through it.'

And so he did, from the first call early last Monday, the morning after Bernie had been taken to hospital, through all the steps of the investigation, stopping every now and then to ask, 'Are you with me?'

Finally, the chilling story was there in front of me — the old man's past as a resistance fighter and poet in Poland; Harry's abusive childhood; the impulsive killing; the discovery of the mallet; Harry's torching of the Clifton Hill house; and his confession.

I was stunned, but details began to fit together. Harry had never told us anything about his childhood. He looked a little foreign, but his surname, Stanley, was Anglo-Australian. When Alison was born he had agreed with Bernadette that she would take her mother's surname.

I didn't know what to feel — grief for Alison; grief for Harry; sadness that our poor dysfunctional family had another tragedy to face. After all these years I found that I was longing for Mum. She would soothe us all with her practical kindness.

'God, Trent, how am I going to explain this to the Judge? And Alison?'

'I'll tell Alison tonight. The Judge is your problem.'

CHAPTER 28
ALISON BRENNAN
SATURDAY 16 APRIL

THIS WAS HOW I FELT. I WAS STANDING AT THE TOP OF A HIGH cliff, and I could hear the sea below, crashing on treacherous rocks.

I wanted to fall off that cliff and never think about anything ever again. It was like I was hanging from my life by a thin thread, and when it broke, I would spin into an abyss and get lost forever. I was a spectator on my own life, looking at it from the outside, while everything happened to someone else.

Everything had gone upside down, sideways and in an out, and over itself so that I couldn't sort anything out anymore. It was like I'd broken through into another world where the people looked the same but were entirely different. It was like I would never, never ever be normal. I would be scared and lonely forever.

Dad, why didn't you tell us?

I HAD a Polish grandfather who wrote poems. He was my dad's father. He was here in Melbourne and he was homeless. My dad killed him and now he's going to jail.

It was like trying to figure out a jigsaw. Trent told me everything last night and warned me that it would be in the newspapers and on the news. The story should have made sense. I knew about refugees coming to Australia after the Second World War, and I thought I knew Dad had a Polish background, but not once did he say anything about his parents or his childhood. And I didn't ask. He was just Dad and he made me think that his life had begun with me and Mum — that he had no life before us. We were an isolated little unit locked away in that horrible house.

The house had burned down. Trent said that Dad set it alight just before they arrested him. I wished I'd been there to see it. I hated that house. It made me feel dirty, secretive, terrified that people would find out how bad it was.

I didn't know where I was and where I was going to go to from here.

Why did Dad never tell me about his father? Why did he kill him? We're not that triangle anymore — Mum, Dad and me. I'm the only point of the triangle left.

CHAPTER 29

COLIN BRENNAN

SATURDAY, 16 APRIL

So now we knew where Harry was, hiding out after he killed his father. Didn't even know he had a father. He never said a word about his family, never said a word about anything. He was very slow and completely dumbstruck when I was around. Then he ran off with Bernadette. How much did he tell her?

I remembered those years after the war. The 'reffos', as we called them, streamed into the country from Europe. Pictures were all over the papers and newsreels in the cinemas —pale, starved, desperate people. We knew nothing of what they'd been through, the horror of it.

It wasn't until much later, studying History at university, that I learnt something of what a bloodbath it had been. The Australian Government sent the poor blighters off to the big hydroelectricity schemes. They lived in bush camps, cutting down virgin forest, building massive dams. Lived lonely, rough, outdoor lives.

So that was Harry's story. Raised in the bush by his father, who was one of the very few survivors of the Polish Home Army, and he was so damaged by what he'd seen that he was probably almost insane. But a fine poet, Leo told me, historically important.

What a disaster! Bernadette's in hospital with another breakdown, Harry's confessed to manslaughter and will go to jail for years. And what about Alison?

Leo apologised a little sheepishly for what he said to me last Monday, about my deficient parenting in regard to Bernadette. I accepted his apology but didn't say much. While we were on the subject of history, perhaps there was some of my own I needed to examine.

We'd have to bury the poor old fellow, of course. So I decided to stay in the city for a while until that was done, and we could sort out some arrangements for Alison.

CHAPTER 30
ALISON BRENNAN
MONDAY, 18 APRIL

I WAS SWIMMING LAPS EARLY, MY MIND FULL OF DAD. MY stroke was fast and automatic, my shoulder muscles were burning and my heart rate was high, but I didn't stop until I'd gone into that space where there was no more thought, just me, the water, and the air I pulled into my lungs.

The memories were like images in a television advertisement, each imposed quickly on the other. I had to watch them to the end, and then maybe I could understand. Dad first brought me to this pool when I was a baby. He loved to tell me how I took to the water immediately, how excited I was when we walked through the door and I knew I was going for my swimming lesson.

My first conscious memory was of when I was four, and we'd come to the pool after kinder. I was kicking on a paddleboard with the other kids, and Dad was standing at the side of the pool, smiling, eyes only for me. When the lesson was over, he lifted me out gently and dried and dressed me, all the time keeping up what I came to think of as 'Daddy talk'.

'Good girl, you swim fast, smart girl. Gonna be an Olympian. Gonna swim for Australia.'

Then I graduated to the squads. No more exercises in the

learning pool, but swimming laps with my age group, always stretching to be the fastest and the strongest, to swim further than all the others. Dad was there every time, never missed a session. 'Good girl, Allie, doing well, love, keep it up.' Every win, every award was for him, my dad.

When I joined the swimming team in Year Seven, I started early morning lap sessions and soon began mixing them up with gym workouts. Dad drove me every morning and waited while I swam or worked out, then showered and dressed. We'd have coffee and something to eat together then he'd drop me at school.

Then by Year Nine I didn't want him coming anymore. I could get to the pool and then to school without him, I told him. 'There's no need, Dad, have a sleep-in.' I knew it hurt him, but I was fourteen and embarrassed by his big, dark presence shadowing me every morning, so obviously proud of me, his spotlight shining just on me. I hated the attention. I wanted to be anonymous.

Dad couldn't read very well. He told me that he grew up without a mother, and his father didn't make him go to school. That was all he'd ever told me about his family. So from the time I learnt to read, in my Prep year, I'd read to him.

He'd be waiting when I came home from school, and he'd go to my bag to pull out my next reader or storybook, to hunt in my library bag for the books I'd borrowed. 'What have we got today, Allie?' Then he'd make me a sandwich and we'd find a place to sit close together. I'd read to him, slowly at first, pointing and sounding out each word. Later the stories were longer and more complicated, and my reading more fluent, but that time was always ours, Dad's and mine.

I never thought, ever, that he didn't love me. He loved me almost too much. He gloried in me. I knew that sounded over the top, but everything he had ever done for me and said to me had told me that I was a miracle in his life. When I was small and fussy with my breakfast, he'd put the sweet, diced, dried fruits that I liked at the bottom of my porridge bowl so that I had to eat it all to find them. He'd brush my hair and plait it for school, and then he'd strap me into his big old car and drop me at the gate. 'See you soon, beautiful girl,' he'd say every morning as he kissed me.

Mum began to get worse when I was in Grade Four. Until then she was messy and very shy, but she'd still leave the house when she had to. But that year it was always Dad and me. He took me everywhere — swimming, school, shopping, and to play in the park. Mum never came. I could see how it happened that they didn't enrol me in a secondary school.

Dad wouldn't have understood. He would have thought it was automatic. Hardly ever having been at school himself, he wouldn't have known how it worked. Mum would have had it vaguely in her mind, that it had to be done, but she was forgetful by then, and housebound. She would have put it off over and over until it was too late and Grandpa had to step in.

When I was older, Dad and I would go to the movies together on Saturday afternoons. 'What's it going to be today, Allie?' he'd ask, and I'd choose a movie that he'd like. We'd buy popcorn and munch happily in the dark, then dissect the movie over milkshakes afterwards. Dad seemed slow because he didn't talk much, but he always talked with me. He loved those movie afternoons, and so did I. They were markers in our week, an excuse to get out of that horrible house.

The last movie we saw together was on the Saturday before I went to Golden Beach for the holidays. It was *Hell or Highwater,* just the kind of movie Dad liked — little guys robbing banks to save the family farm. We had Chinese afterwards, and we ordered extra in a takeaway container for Mum. I felt close to him, so that was why I told him that I was going to Grandpa's house for the holidays, before telling Mum.

'Good on you, love,' he had said, covering my hand with

his. 'It'll do you good to get away. Don't tell Mum until the day you're going. She'll get into a state.'

Dad knew it wasn't right, the way we were living, but I didn't think he knew what to do about it.

He had never hurt me, not once, but I had seen him get uncontrollably angry. The anger seemed to come from nowhere and it raged for a minute or two then it died away. When he was angry like that, I didn't think he was aware of what he was doing.

One time there was a TV show on late that Mum wanted to watch. He said he'd record it for her. When she turned on the TV to watch it the next day, the show hadn't recorded and she was disappointed.

'You told me you'd tape it, Harry,' she wailed. She was like a spoiled child sometimes.

Then something happened to Dad. He picked up the TV and dropped it, pushed it over, stomped on it and kicked and kicked it until it was in pieces. Mum and I just stood there, our mouths open, staring.

'Dad, stop,' I called, but he didn't seem to hear me.

Then the rage was over. He picked up the pieces of the TV and threw them into the front yard. When I started to say something about it to Mum, she put her finger to her lips. Leave it alone.

The next day when I came home from school there was a big new TV in the place where the old one had been.

There were other times too, but never directed at me, and I never saw him hurt Mum. Sometimes I'd hear him out in his shed shouting and throwing things around, upturning old boxes, kicking at the walls, swearing. One time I heard him crying like a broken-hearted child. 'Let him be,' Mum had said. She told me to stay away from him when he was like that.

Dad, I know you love me. I can tell you things and you listen. Mum told me that there was a lot of bad stuff in your childhood, but you never talk about it. I understand why. You wanted me to be a new beginning. You didn't want me touched by it. But I am now because you're in jail. I can't escape your past any more than you can.

There were so many thoughts I wanted to share with Dad, so I wrote him a letter.

Dear Dad,

Whatever you did and why ever you did it, you're still my dad and I love you. I'm staying at Uncle Leo's. Mum's in hospital and I haven't seen her yet. I don't know what's going on, and I can't think straight about anything, but I know you're a good and kind person. Nothing will make me stop believing that.

Trent said he'd make sure you get this note. He said that maybe I can see you soon.

Your loving daughter, Alison.

CHAPTER 31
COLIN BRENNAN
WEDNESDAY, 20 APRIL

As funerals went, it wasn't exactly the event of the year. It was a short, simple service at St Francis Church in the city, and then on to the cemetery. There weren't many of us — Trent and his colleague Jossie, with an old gentleman she introduced as her grandfather; Alison in her school uniform keeping very close to Leo; a Polish woman Trent said was Professor Nadia Godlewski from Melbourne University; and two friends of the deceased, Bett and Stu. And of course me, wondering how I got to be there, on such a dreary Melbourne day, watching as a stranger's coffin was lowered into the ground.

Then suddenly, as the sun broke through and outlined the scene in gold, a clear, strong contralto voice broke into song behind me. I could tell it was a prayer. It began softly, reverently, and then it climbed to a crescendo, culminating in the word 'Jezus', and then in rich, deep tones it descended again to 'Amen'.

I looked at Trent who was standing near me with Jossie and her grandfather. The old man was trembling, holding tightly to his walking stick.

'It's the *Hail Mary* in Polish,' Jossie whispered.

Nadia Godlewski sang the prayer of Borys Stasiewicz's boyhood three times, as each of us threw handfuls of Australian dirt onto the coffin. The song was deeply, sweetly melodic, full of emotion — a song of pride and grief, but also of hope and endurance.

What an extraordinary woman, I thought, *to do such a perfect thing.*

Then it was over and Borys was laid to rest, with a dignity that life had not always afforded him.

CHAPTER 32
ALISON BRENNAN
WEDNESDAY, 20 APRIL

I STILL HAD THE STRANGE SENSATION OF BEING OUTSIDE OF MY life. It was as if the girl standing there with Leo in that cold cemetery was someone who, although she looked exactly like me, was a ghost. The real me looked on unfeeling, from somewhere high above.

Then the sun came out and that Professor began to sing in a deep strong voice, a prayer I didn't understand. She began softly and then her voice grew and soared, and it was beautiful. She sang as we threw earth onto my grandfather's coffin, and somehow that prayer and her deep, unusual voice gave the sad scene a feeling of something big and deep.

When the funeral was over and we were about to leave, she came to me and took both my hands in hers. She seemed to want to hold them forever. 'Borys Stasiewicz's granddaughter!' she said, looking hard into my eyes.

I looked right back. *I'm going to be proud of him*, I thought, *no matter how his life ended.*

'He was a great patriot,' she said, 'a grandfather to boast about … to learn from. Never forget that.'

Grandpa came up then to thank her for coming and they moved away together across the cold grass.

CHAPTER 33
JOSSIE WALLACHIA
WEDNESDAY, 20 APRIL

I ASKED MY GRANDFATHER TO COME WITH ME TO HOBIE'S funeral. After all, he was the one who'd sent us to Nadia with Hobie's poems. He was very frail, but he agreed to come when I promised him lunch at the Polish restaurant in Chapel Street. He almost never got out.

'They were martyrs for Poland,' he said when I told him Hobie's story. 'Hardly any of the soldiers of the Home Army survived. There were no second chances, no trials, just a bullet through the head or a knife through the guts. The fact that he survived Warsaw and made it to Australia is almost miraculous.'

'He was a clever man, Dziadek,' I said. 'He survived as a guerrilla fighter, writing his subversive poetry for at least four years before the uprising. He must have learnt ways to hide his identity.'

Dziadek just nodded.

'What about you, Grandfather?' I asked. 'You never talk about Poland.'

'When you see your country and your beautiful city, its art and culture reduced to rubble, your friends and family murdered, you don't want to talk about it, little one.' He used the Polish endearment, 'Malenka' for 'little one', which he always used for me.

'How did you get out?'

'Your grandmother and I escaped before the worst of it. You see, we had German citizenship. When we knew the Nazis were coming, we fled to Germany, made our way from there to France and finally across the Channel to England. We knew we'd be safe there. After the war, we decided to leave the mess of Europe behind and migrate to Australia. We were the lucky ones …' He looked wistful. 'Or the less brave,' he then added softly.

I took his old, blue-veined hand in mine. 'I'm certainly glad you got out, Dziadek.'

So in that cold cemetery, I put my arm through his as he leaned on his stick, and I thanked whatever kind Spirit had brought him and my grandmother here safely.

When Nadia began to sing, Grandfather became very still. I glanced at him. He was pale, and his face was blank and impassive. Then tears began to roll down his cheeks, staining the warm scarf he wore around his neck.

'What is it, Dziadek?' I whispered.

'We used to sing it after Mass when I was a boy. Three *Hail Marys* for the prosperity and peace of Poland.'

CHAPTER 34
BETT
WEDNESDAY, 20 APRIL

I ALMOST DIDN'T GO; POOR HOBIE WAS LOST TO ME NOW. After I'd identified his body as the person I knew as Herbert Stanley, I wanted it all to end. But the little blonde detective insisted on picking Stu and me up. Her grandfather was with her, a very old man. *God knows what he made of us, the derelicts from the park.*

I'd washed as well as I could in the public toilets, shampooed my hair and cleaned my best jacket and skirt. I'd bought stockings from the 7/11, and I thought I looked presentable enough. It was a short church ceremony, and then out to the graveyard. I was just waiting for it to be over, hoping I wouldn't embarrass myself with tears.

Then I saw the girl, Hobie's granddaughter, and I had to tell myself not to stare. I kept sneaking little glances at her as if to paint her picture in my mind. She was a beautiful creature, slim and straight, an athletic build, long, glossy brown hair and the bluest eyes I'd ever seen. She wore the uniform of that expensive private school on St Kilda Road.

The detective, Jossie, she said to call her, took me over to the girl. I hung back. Living rough did that to you. You lost your confidence.

'Your grandfather's close friend,' Jossie said.

The girl, Alison, looked at me as if she wanted to get inside my head.

'What was he like?' she asked as she shook my hand.

I couldn't answer. *How do you put a lifetime into a few sentences in a cemetery, while staring into a hole in the ground?*

'Come and talk to me one day, dear.' I didn't know why I said that.

'Yes, I will, I will.'

Then the coffin was being lowered and that Polish woman began to sing just as the sun came out. Her deep voice, and the complex consonants of Hobie's mother tongue, with the reverence of a prayer rising and falling in the air, moved me in a way I hadn't felt since listening to the Torah being sung in synagogue.

Suddenly, I was glad for Hobie's life, glad we'd found each other, glad for the beautiful girl, his granddaughter, and glad that she wanted to talk to me.

I threw my little handful of dirt onto Hobie's coffin. It was an ending, but somehow there was also the feeling of a beginning.

CHAPTER 35
COLIN BRENNAN
THURSDAY, 21 APRIL

'ASYLUMS', WE USED TO CALL THEM. BUT THIS WASN'T ONE of those foreboding fortress-like prisons, with a stone façade and high-arched windows. It was streamlined and modern, brightly lit and decorated with stiff-looking designer pitchers of flowers. But it was still unnerving.

The cleanliness and gloss, and the bright voices of the nurses couldn't disguise the blank faces of the few patients who shuffled past the door, or the resigned sobs further down the corridor. A thick carpet minimised noise in the little parlour to which I'd been assigned, but somewhere not far away was the clatter of lunch trays. I waited in silence to meet with Bernadette's psychiatrist, Dr Sarah Soliman.

I longed for the meeting to be over. It was a bad business, and I felt inadequate to handle it. A part of my conscience that I was determined to ignore kept suggesting that I may not be entirely blameless in Bernadette's illness.

When she was hospitalised the first time, Mary dealt with everything, leaving me to bury myself further in my work. I was newly appointed to the bench, and Mary was so competent. When we finally had a name for the condition, I was happy to leave the treatment to the professionals, and Bernadette's continued improvement to Mary.

Leo was in his final year at school, and I didn't want him distracted. And Bernadette did improve. She and her mother would go shopping, and to plays, to the ballet, to charity lunches. Bernadette clung to Mary emotionally, but at least, I told myself, she was no longer locked away in her bedroom. Then Mary's death crushed her again, and she rushed into that unfortunate relationship with the simpleton, Harry.

I was getting fidgety. I wasn't good at waiting, and I hated it when people were late. Then just as I was wondering where the damn woman was, Dr Sarah Soliman arrived. She was small, with medium-length grey hair in that style they called a bob, and she was dressed in a smart grey trouser suit. I towered over her when I rose to greet her. She shook my hand briskly and seated herself in a chair opposite me, all business. She carried a manila folder, which she placed on the low table in front of her.

I took the lead. 'Thank you for seeing me, Dr Soliman. How is Bernadette?'

Sarah Soliman briefly consulted her file.

'It's early days, so her progress is limited but satisfactory for this stage. Our immediate goals are physical. Bernadette needs a regular, healthy diet and the re-establishment of hygiene habits. The nurses make sure she showers every day, and her diet is being monitored. It seems that she was eating very poorly, especially in the weeks leading up to her admission.'

Was she accusing me of something? Surely, as a grown woman, Bernadette could have monitored her own diet. I decided not to respond, and pointed to the overnight bag, which Leo and Alison had filled with nightwear, clothes and toiletries. 'I'd be grateful if you'd see that she gets this,' I said.

'Of course. Now, what can you tell me of her psychiatric history?'

I wondered why she asked that. Surely it was in the file; but that meant consulting with Bernadette's previous psychiatrist, and perhaps he was no longer practising. So I responded with the history of Bernadette's earlier hospitalisation, her relapse when her mother became terminally ill, Alison's birth, and her gradual decline again into agoraphobia. I didn't mention the hoarding. It all seemed far too complicated, and already I was weary of this interview.

'That first hospitalisation when she was twenty-one. Was there a triggering event?'

'What do you mean?'

'Well, anxiety-induced agoraphobia is almost always triggered by a traumatic event, something perhaps that so panicked Bernadette that she didn't want to leave the safety of her bed.'

'I have no idea,' I said. 'I wasn't involved in Bernadette's treatment. My wife looked after everything.'

Sarah Soliman looked at me a little too long for my liking.

'You're a retired Judge, I believe.'

'Yes. How is that relevant?'

She ignored my question and asked another. 'What work were you involved in when Bernadette was first hospitalised?'

'I'd just been appointed to the bench. I was a newly appointed Judge, so very busy, and my wife was extraordinarily competent. I was happy for her to take care of Bernadette.'

'Was your wife happy with that? Would she have liked you to have been more involved?'

I could feel sweat on my forehead and under my collar. This nosy, bloody woman was beginning to annoy me. 'My wife was very supportive of my work and understood the burdens it imposed on my time.'

'I see.'

There it was again, that look that lingered a little too long.

I tried to get back on the forward foot. 'What's the treatment for the condition, Dr Soliman?'

'We approach the treatment in a number of ways. First the nursing staff will look to the patient's physical needs and institute a program to promote general good health. They encourage patients to take part in activities in the unit and to mix with other patients to the extent that they are able.'

I had a sudden vision of Bernadette weaving baskets and making clay pots, and almost laughed. She couldn't manage even the simplest tasks, and she never communicated with anyone. 'Drugs?' I asked.

'Yes, agoraphobia patients are initially treated with mood-stabilising drugs, and it can take time to establish which of these and in which combinations are right for the individual. I've started Bernadette on a mild anti-depressant, but that will be assessed as her therapy gets underway. That's really the most important part of the treatment, the talk therapy.'

'How long will that take?'

'It's impossible to say. Bernadette is very traumatised. We use talk therapy to try to discover the basis of the trauma, to help the patient to acknowledge and understand it, and in time, to end the hold it has over her psychological health. It could take weeks or months, but you need to understand that even after she leaves, she will need regular sessions with a psychiatrist and strong support from her family.'

'I see.'

What more bloody support does she need, I wondered. *I'm already paying for this expensive private hospital, and Bernadette's made it clear in the past that she doesn't want a bar of me.*

'With your permission, I'd like some more information about the circumstances of Bernadette's admission.'

'I wasn't there, Dr Soliman. I was informed the following morning.'

'Oh yes, I see now. She was admitted by her brother. I

have those details here. But again, what do you know about what precipitated the crisis?'

'I only know what my son has told me. My granddaughter returned from a two-week holiday with me to find her mother bedridden, unwashed and irrational. There was no water to the house and she refused to leave her bed. My granddaughter called my son, a CAT team attended and she was brought here.'

'Something must have brought it on though.'

'It seems that it was the fact that my granddaughter left her to spend the two weeks of the school holidays with me at Golden Beach. Bernadette saw it as a betrayal, called Alison a traitor, and screamed at her to leave the house.'

'Why would Alison taking a holiday with you be seen by Bernadette as betrayal?'

'We don't exactly have a close, loving relationship, but I admit I don't understand why she loathes me so much.'

'Hmm,' was all the insufferable woman said.

There was a silence, which I interpreted as accusatory, and I made up my mind to bring the interview to a close. 'Well, if that's all, Dr Soliman.'

She wasn't going to let me go easily. 'For the time being,' she said, 'but it's going to be central to the therapy that we understand the cause of the original breakdown when she was younger.'

'As I've said, I know nothing about it.'

'Well, we'll no doubt find out more from her previous psychiatrist, but there definitely would have been a triggering event.'

'The death of her mother, of course. Bernadette was very dependent on her.'

'Yes, but that was later, wasn't it? That was the cause of the re-appearance of the agoraphobia, but what brought on the initial breakdown when she was twenty-one?'

Why does she keep harping on this? 'As I've said, I don't know.'

'I believe that the re-emergence of Bernadette's agoraphobia was probably caused by her mother's illness and death, but it can also be a reaction or a defiant act against an intimidating, critical or bullying spouse or parent. In Bernadette's case it's far too early to say if that's the case.'

The damn woman actually looked me straight in the eye when she said that.

'In any case, there's a lot of work to be done. Thank you for coming.' She then rose, the diminutive bully, and shook my hand again.

'Thank you, Dr Soliman, here's my card. Please contact me immediately if I can be of further assistance.'

I wasn't going to ask if and when we could see Bernadette. It would only risk another of her cold stares.

I left feeling like one of those schoolboys who couldn't quite be trusted, the one every teacher had on a watch list, a recalcitrant child, resistant to discipline who might make terrible trouble if left unchecked.

In the so-called 'talk therapy', I knew who the villain would be.

As I walked out through those spotless corridors, I realised that while I now had some technical information about Bernadette's illness, I still had no understanding, nothing but the familiar lurch of desolation curling like a watery wave in my belly. I felt old and useless, and I thought I might weep.

In my pocket my fingers skimmed the keypad of my phone, urging me to do it, to dial Nadia's number, to seek out her calm presence. However, I — the feared Judge Colin Brennan of the criminal court — was afraid of her rejection. And even worse, I was afraid of her pity.

CHAPTER 36
ALISON BRENNAN
MONDAY, 25 APRIL

I DECIDED TO GO TO SCHOOL. LEO WANTED ME TO TAKE TIME off, but I didn't want to get too behind with my work. The only day I took off was for my grandfather's funeral last Wednesday.

At lunchtime, I was in the library, drifting around, trying to hide. I was out of my body, as if the girl doing things wasn't me, but a stranger who looked like me. I felt like a snail carrying a shell that was much too heavy. The shell could crack and squash me any moment. I couldn't give my attention to anything except the weight on my back.

It was funny that the worst thing about the whole thing was also the best thing. Worst, because no one else knew, except Grandpa, Leo and Trent, and now Mrs Goodall, because Leo had asked me if he could phone the school and tell her.

I could never tell Rosa, ever. Nothing weird or shameful like this happened in her family. She'd look at me as if I was some strange, alien species. That was also the best thing. Because no one else at school knew (except Mrs Goodall), I didn't *have* to talk about it. Everyone expected me to be normal. They couldn't see the heavy shell that sat on my back waiting to crush me.

But when have I ever been normal?

I was the neglected little girl from the dirty house, remember? They wouldn't let me see Mum, and Dad was in the Melbourne Assessment Centre waiting for his trial. Trent said he'd probably go to jail, but he didn't know for how long. Trent was going to find out when I could see Dad.

I sat next to Rosa in English Literature class every day, but I made excuses when she suggested doing stuff at the weekend. She looked hurt, and I hated that. I thought she'd just give up on me.

But what can I do? I can't tell her. She wouldn't believe even half of it.

It hurt to smile with this heaviness around me, so I stopped trying. I wished I could run away and hide forever. That was probably what happened to Mum. Something drove her to her hiding place. But no, I wouldn't be my mother.

Everyone at school was talking about assignments, shopping at the weekends, posting on social media, sending texts.

They think it all matters, but it doesn't.

CHAPTER 37
STELLA GOODALL
MONDAY, 25 APRIL

What a day!

A stream of sad, angry, confused and questioning kids. More teachers than usual wanted to talk about students' behaviours ranging from the merely challenging to the downright dangerous — ridiculous amounts of paperwork; the Year Twelve boy shaken with grief after taking his girlfriend for an abortion during the holidays; the Year Ten girl who had to shut down her Facebook page because of a spiteful vendetta from her classmates; and the artistic boy who wanted to be a dancer, not the doctor his parents hoped for.

I was trying to be present to each concern as fully as I could. Trying to listen because listening was the first act of healing.

Then there was Alison's story.

She came this morning, diffident and quiet, looking as if all the darkness in the world sat on her shoulders. I knew the bare outline from her uncle. First, I had to make sure she had somewhere safe to stay, and I assured her that she and her uncle had done the best thing for her mother.

Then the story came out in fits and starts. There was still a lot that Alison didn't understand; how her father had kept his background secret for so long; the full story of her Polish grandfather's escape to Australia; and the angry memories that led her father to kill his own father. She didn't know yet what was going to happen to her father, and at least for the time being her mother was lost to her.

This was a girl desperately in need of calm, responsible parenting, and there was no one to provide it. She had built a shell, as children did who saw themselves as different and inferior. The shell was her self-sufficiency, but underneath that confident self-containment, she was lonely. She stepped carefully through the world, always conscious to minimise the risk that her secrets would be revealed.

Somewhere along the way, however, she had learnt to be kind, even learnt to love. Despite their many faults as parents, she instinctively defended her mother and father. There was a goodness in Alison that belied her circumstances.

Where did it come from? Are there people who are naturally good, despite adversity? Alison is a mystery to me. Her resilience raises many questions that I can't answer. But I do know this. While her emotional strength will no doubt at times add to her loneliness, it will also be her salvation into a better future.

I urged her to see herself as her own parent, nurturing and taking care of herself, of her own emotional needs. I asked her to imagine her emotional self as a small child, a child in great need of love and comfort. What exactly did such a child need, I asked? Then I asked her to imagine the rational, logical part of herself as a parent to that child. She must 'parent' herself, I suggested.

'How do I do that,' she asked.

I asked her to think about what good parents did. They provided good food and a healthy environment; they gave affirmation and unconditional love. They made sure that their child had good social connections, friends, and pleasant things to look forward to; simple things like a swim on a hot day, a story or good book, a funny movie to watch, time to play, to talk and dream, and to be happy in the moment.

Alison stared at me with those navy blue eyes, but I knew she understood. I asked her to call into my office every day, even just for a moment, and tell me one loving thing she had done for herself in the last twenty-four hours. The situation would unfold without her, but this was a way she could care for her own needs and retain some control.

When she went back to class, I remembered her grandfather, the rather forbidding retired Judge who paid her school fees and whom I'd seen in the distance at Parent Information nights. She needed more than that now. She needed emotional nurturing, and someone grown-up to talk to. Perhaps it was time Judge Brennan became more involved in Alison's life.

CHAPTER 38
LEO BRENNAN
SATURDAY, 30 APRIL

The doctor had warned us not to expect much. 'Bernadette is still very withdrawn,' she'd said. 'It's going to take time.'

Bernadette looked fresh and clean. Her gold-grey hair stood in curls around her head, just as I remembered it from when she was younger. She wore a dressing gown and slippers and sat in an armchair by the window. There was a view across the rooves of the suburb, but Bernie wasn't looking at it. Across her knees was a portable table, and on it she played some kind of card game. She hardly looked up when we came in.

'Hello Bernie,' I said, kissing her on the cheek. 'How are you?'

She looked at me as if trying to work out who I was, and then she returned to her cards. Did she recall that Sunday evening when Alison found her stinking and huddled in bed, with no water to the house? Did she remember the CAT team coming? Did she remember how she scratched and fought? Did she blame me for admitting her to this hospital? If she did, she didn't say anything about it. She just kept on sorting and stacking those damn cards in some endless game of Patience.

Then Alison bent to kiss her. I couldn't imagine how hard it must have been for her to see her mother like this. She pulled up a chair next to Bernie and tried to take her hand, but Bernie wouldn't give up the cards. 'How are you, Mum?' she asked, but there was no response, just the slap of the cards as Bernie thumped them onto the table.

We waited for a few moments, prepared to sit with her even if she chose to ignore us. I wondered if she realised who Alison was, but then, still holding her cards, she turned to her daughter and asked very formally. 'How is school going, dear?' It was as if she'd been practising conversational openers.

But it was something. It gave Alison the opening to chatter about teachers, assignments, and sport. I could see her trying her utmost to engage her mother's interest.

'Oh Mum, remember that swimming teacher I told you about …?'

'Mum, did I tell you about the brilliant novel we're studying this term?'

'I met this girl called Rosa. She's funny. I went to her house. Her father's a chef and her mother makes beautiful clothes.'

'Can I bring you some books to read, Mum, maybe some magazines? Would you like some DVDs?'

None of this provoked any visible interest in Bernie. She made non-committal noises and kept turning over and sorting her cards.

At least this is a start, I thought, wondering if she'd ask about Harry. We'd been told not to bring up anything that would upset her, so I was prepared to lie and say that we knew nothing about him, but she didn't ask. The Judge had attended court to hear Harry plead guilty to the manslaughter of his father, and from him and what had been reported in the papers, we knew the basic facts. I had a clipping in my wallet, but this was certainly not the time to reveal it to Bernie.

Yesterday in the Supreme Court of Victoria, Henryk Stanley pleaded guilty to the manslaughter of homeless man Borys Staskiewicz, who was killed in Enterprise Park, Melbourne, early on the morning of Monday, 11 April. Acting on behalf of Stanley, Legal Aid barrister Patricia Coulihan proffered that Staskiewicz was Stanley's father, and that the two had had a troubled relationship since Stanley's childhood.

Stanley did not intend to kill Stasiewicz, Coulihan argued, but had gone to the park to check on his safety. An argument ensued, in the course of which Stanley flew into a rage, grabbed the mallet that Staskiewicz kept by his side and bashed him on the side of the head causing his death.

Stanley wore a dark hoodie and track pants and stood impassively in the dock. He did not seek bail and will return to court in May for sentencing.

The report was accompanied by a drawing of Harry, the familiar long, lank hair parted to either side of his face, his large features expressionless.

I didn't know why I had cut out that clipping. Perhaps I hoped that one day Bernie would be well and we could talk about the events as the close brother and sister we once were.

Alison and I sat for about twenty minutes, each of us searching for a topic that might distract or amuse her, each of us blabbing against her disinterest.

And then finally, it was time to go. We were not to tire her, the stern head nurse had said.

I kissed Bernie, saying, 'Get well, darling,' and turned to the door.

Then Alison bent to kiss her mother.

'I'll come often, Mum, whenever I can,' she promised. She moved away from Bernie's chair, despondent. Then she turned back. 'I love you, Mum, please get better.' She touched her mother's face gently, and then she joined me at the door.

CHAPTER 39
ALISON BRENNAN
SATURDAY, 7 MAY

YESTERDAY, OUR SCIENCE CLASS WENT ON AN EXCURSION — Melbourne Aquarium in the morning and Scienceworks in the afternoon. Even I was excited to get away from the classroom. Rosa climbed into the bus right after me and sat in the seat beside me. I smiled at her, and then turned my head to look out the window. I was embarrassed that I'd been distant with her.

'You can't stop me sitting here,' she said.

Then, after a few seconds, she tried again, saying, 'Talk to me Allie, please.' She held up a plastic container, opening the lid a little. A delicious smell leaked out. 'Look, Dad made Thai fish cakes with satay sauce last night. I've brought enough for the two of us for lunch. I'm happy to bribe you with food if nothing else works.'

Trent had put a packet of cheese sandwiches into my bag as I left that morning, but I so wanted to share those fish cakes with Rosa. I wanted to tell her some of what was going on, but I couldn't. If she knew everything, she'd never want to speak to me again. She might even tell other kids at school and the look of normality that I'd built up would be blown. I'd have to leave the school.

'I'm sorry, Rosa,' I said. 'I don't want to hurt you.' I could feel the hot tears coming and my face contorted as I tried to control them. 'It's just that stuff's happening in my family, horrible stuff that I can't tell anyone. My mum's sick in hospital, but that's just the beginning. If you knew everything that's going on, you'd hate me.'

'Why would I hate you?'

'Because your family's perfect.'

Rosa stared at me, her eyes wide. Then she said, 'Is that what you think? My family is definitely *not* perfect. Why do you think we moved from Sydney? Family stuff! Dad's business failed and Mum had an affair. For months I hated them both. There was fighting all the time. Mum was never home, and I had to look after Gio. I had to be a mother to him. I hated her most of all for that. The move down here was to try to make a new start.'

'I'm sorry,' I said. I didn't know any of that. 'But you live in that gorgeous house.'

'That gorgeous *rented* house. Dad went bankrupt. I still don't know if they'll stay together, and Gio's had to leave his school and his friends. No, my family's far from perfect. Anyway, this stuff in your family. Is it your fault? What? Are you dealing drugs? Do you have a secret bikie boyfriend who cooks ice?'

'Noooo.' I laughed.

'Well, if it's not your fault, why does it have to stop you being friends with me? Heaps of kids have shit in their families. I could tell you some stuff you wouldn't believe about kids at my old school.'

'You wouldn't believe my stuff either.' I stared out of the window, trying to will the tears not to come.

'I don't know why you think I care about that. I'm not planning to adopt your family. It was cool when we hung out that Saturday. Didn't we have fun?'

'Yes, we did.' I remembered that day, how I'd forgotten to worry for a few hours.

'So what's the problem?'

'There's a lot of stuff I can't talk about,' I said again.

'I totally get that. I'm okay with it. Look, do you want to share my fish cakes or shall I offer them to Princess Selma?'

'Don't you dare.' The cheese sandwiches could wait.

She leant across and hugged me, and then I fanned my face to cool down the redness from my tears. By the time we reached the Aquarium, no one would have known that I'd been crying.

I'm letting myself have a friend.

Mrs Goodall's voice had been in my head, reminding me how I needed to be a parent to myself. So Rosa and I spent today together again at her house. It was fun. We painted each other's toenails, and experimented with makeup again while we watched YouTube 'how to' tutorials. We danced to Taylor Swift and Christina Aguilera videos, and Rosa made me try on some of her clothes.

We have different tastes. I'm the jeans and shirt type, but she likes to glam her clothes up. She has glitzy tops and skirts that her mum makes for her. On her they look fabulous, but on me they just look weird.

It was heavy football season. Today Carlton and Collingwood played each other at the MCG. Rosa was a Collingwood barracker, so we watched the game, in between making cupcakes in the kitchen and Rosa plaiting my hair. After his soccer game, Gio came home with Rosa's mum, and we iced the cupcakes and ate some of them as Carlton beat Collingwood.

Just before the end of the game, Rosa's older brother, Dario, came home. Last year we studied the Tennessee Williams play *A Streetcar Named Desire*, and then we watched the 1951 movie with Vivien Leigh and Marlon Brando. In that movie, Marlon Brando was beautiful. People didn't usually use that word about men, but 'handsome' didn't fit. Brando's face *was* beautiful. Later, I watched *The Wild One* and my crush was complete, at least until it moved on to Justin Bieber and Jaden Smith.

Dario looked exactly like Marlon Brando in those films, sort of dark and brooding, rough and sexy. He had perfect features, dark eyes and thick eyebrows, with wavy, black hair and full lips. His face was perfectly symmetrical, and like Brando, he looked as if he couldn't be trusted. He wore a tight T-shirt that showed his chest and arm muscles. He went into the kitchen to get food and then stood watching the game, eating his sandwich. I was suddenly shy and tongue-tied, although he didn't take any notice of us.

When the game was over, when Carlton had won by three goals, and when Rosa had put her head in her hands in pretend despair, I stood to leave.

'I'll come with you to the tram stop,' Rosa volunteered.

Suddenly, Dario said, 'Do you want a lift?'

Rosa cut in, 'No, she's cool, Dario.'

'Thanks anyway,' I said.

He shrugged his shoulders. 'See you then.'

TOMORROW WAS MOTHER'S DAY. I was going to ask Grandpa to give me a photo of my grandmother, and I was going to frame it and put in on her desk in my room at Leo's house. I didn't know if or when I'd ever have a room of my own again, but that was what I had for now. I was going to take flowers to Mum and sit with her for an hour, even if she wouldn't talk to me.

Next Saturday, Rosa was coming to Leo's house and we were going to watch all four episodes of *A Year in the Life* on Netflix.

CHAPTER 40
COLIN BRENNAN
MONDAY, 9 MAY

NADIA GODLEWSKI. THERE WAS A STILLNESS ABOUT HER, A quality of restfulness. She seemed like a thinker. When she sang the three *Hail Marys* in Polish at Stasiewicz's funeral, I was awed by the rightness of the gift, and by her reverence.

Three *Hail Marys*. That's what you got for Penance as a child after you confessed your paltry misdeeds. The *Hail Mary* was the older Catholic's prayer. Kids didn't know those traditional prayers nowadays, didn't know anything about religion, even if they had been baptised. But really, the church hadn't covered itself in glory recently. Priests were in jail for sexually abusing children, another lot were leaving to marry, then some of the younger ones were running around in cassocks as if it was still the 1950s, and Vatican II never happened. I was tired of it all, but I wasn't going to give it up. I was not a quitter. I'd stay to the end on the off-chance that there was a heaven and that the church might know something about it.

Nadia Godlewski. A solid woman, not young, she occupied her space confidently but quietly — very Polish in the features, wide-open face and thick, dark curly hair to her shoulders.

Old fool that I am, I'm attracted to her. There you are, I've said it. I haven't been interested in any woman since Mary died almost twenty years ago. I don't know anything about her. She's probably married. A woman like that would be.

After that interview with Bernadette's doctor, I felt like a whipped dog. I looked for a hole where I could lick my wounds. I wanted to hide, from myself as much as from other people. The loneliness and self-doubt were too common now. I hadn't given way to them before. I wanted to go home to Golden Beach and my solitary existence, but we had to sort something out for Alison first. I was not leaving her with Bernadette again.

I rang Nadia Godlewski, feeling like a teenager, afraid of rejection.

What an act of courage it is, I thought, *to put yourself forward, to offer yourself like this.*

I called her at the university, almost hoping she wouldn't be there and I could put the ordeal off for another day. But she answered, in that clear, slightly accented, deeply layered voice.

'Professor Godlewski. It's Colin Brennan. We met at Borys Stasiewicz's funeral.'

'Oh!'

Was there surprise? Curiosity?

'How are you, Judge Brennan?'

'Well, thank you. Please call me Colin, and may I call you Nadia?'

'Of course.'

Thank God, I breathed out. The immediate formalities were over. 'I wonder how busy you are. I have some questions about Borys Stasiewicz, and Harry, Alison's father. You know of course that he's confessed to manslaughter.'

'Yes, I know that.'

I was stumbling now. *Don't blather,* I warned myself. 'I know very little about Poland and the war. Alison's distraught about her father, and I thought if I understood Stasiewicz's background better, I could talk with her about it.'

'You're close to Alison?'

'Because of her family situation, we were estranged for a time, but I'm trying to make up for that.'

'Yes, I understand. I'm happy to help.'

'I wondered if we could have lunch one day this week.' I waited as if on a knife edge. I'd know immediately if she thought I was a nuisance.

She hesitated slightly, and then she said, 'That would be pleasant. Just checking my diary. Yes, tomorrow would be good, but somewhere close, I have students in the afternoon.'

So we settled on one of those ubiquitous Italian restaurants on Lygon Street, one to which she could walk from the university.

I wanted to run in circles with excitement.

OUR CONVERSATION FELT NATURAL IMMEDIATELY. I had no idea what I ate or drank, but I knew that I listened. She wore a long black cape for the cold day, draping it casually across the back of her chair, and I was captivated. I took everything in hungrily — her scholarship, her humanity and her intuition.

She spoke of the brutality of the German occupation of Poland. 'More wicked than we can ever imagine or describe,' she said. 'There were no rules. Whole families were shot on sight and their land taken. It was quite systematic. The Germans wanted to rid Poland of its people, because the land was paramount to Germany's plans for expansion. As they murdered the Poles or dragged them off to camps, they moved Germans into the homes and farms.'

'Where was Stasiewicz in this?'

Nadia sipped the one glass of wine she had allowed herself. 'There are two things to know about Borys Stasiewicz,' she said. 'First, he was a young intellectual and a prominent poet. He taught at the university of Warsaw until the Germans closed it, but then he continued his writing and teaching in secret. The apartment he shared with his wife, Maria, in Warsaw, was a meeting place for young activists, all of whom were writing patriotic material and taking on the Germans in whatever ways they could.'

'Oh, he was married then?'

'Yes, it was Maria who collected and printed the writings of the Generation of Columbus, as they called themselves. She printed Borys's poems, distributing about thirty copies among the group. One of those was found in his possession. It's an extremely important find and it must be preserved. I wonder where it is now.'

'Still in evidence until Harry's sentenced, I suppose. What happed to Maria?'

'Gunned down in the 1944 uprising. She was pregnant with their first child.' Nadia ate silently, picking at her pasta.

What sadists we humans are, I thought, *and so greedy for power.* 'What was the second factor about Stasiewicz?'

'At a certain point he became a guerrilla fighter. There were a number of different groups that formed the Home Army, basically a loose militia that was loyal to the Polish government, which was in exile in London. They took on the Germans, in the forests mainly, and they were very involved in the sabotage of German transport and weapons. Then in 1944, they staged the uprising in Warsaw and most were mowed down.' Nadia's voice was full of grief, and I realised that, as a Pole, this terrible history was also hers.

'I wonder how Stasiewicz escaped.'

'That's a mystery. Almost no Home Army soldiers survived the uprising. Somehow he must have mingled in with the thousands being sent to camps, and when the camps were liberated by the Allies, they joined the mass of refugees to Australia. Until now no Polish historian knew he was here.'

"What about Harry? Why would he attack his father like that?'

Nadia finished her pasta and sipped the last of her wine, considering the question.

'This is an educated guess. Borys would have been psychologically damaged from all that he'd endured. Put yourself in his shoes. Displaced from his country, his wife murdered before his eyes, lost without a history or a name in this huge, puzzling country, and assigned rough work in harsh conditions. He was an intellectual, a poet. Then there was the sense of grievance against the West, a belief that the Allies had let Poland down. And there was resentfulness that the Russian army hadn't intervened when Germany took Poland, even though it was just outside Poland's borders. All that anger, combined with dispossession. It seems that he was an alcoholic, and possibly a violent and neglectful father.'

'But for Harry to bash him like that in an uncontrollable fury.'

'Colin,' Nadia said, putting down her glass. 'We'll never know what that boy suffered. But whatever his faults as a father, for his contribution to Polish literature, Borys Stasiewicz deserves respect and for his memory to be preserved.'

It was such a pleasure to be with this intelligent woman. We spoke for longer, of happier things, of her work and her family.

'I came to Australia in 1952, with my parents. I was three years old. They were part of the massive exodus from Europe after the war. First we lived with relatives and then my parents found a house in Carnegie, which they rented for the rest of their lives. My father was a doctor in Poland, but his qualifications weren't recognised here, so he worked all of his life as a hospital orderly.' She smiled grimly, and I recalled other stories I had heard of gifted, educated refugees being forced to work in menial jobs.

'What about your mother?' I asked.

'She was a celebrated concert pianist in Poland, but in

Australia she spent her days giving children piano lessons. She never performed again.'

We were silent for a moment, and then Nadia said, 'They were marvellous people. They died within days of each other ten years ago.'

'Were you their only child?'

'Yes, my parents valued education so I was expected to work hard and achieve at school. In primary school I was educated by an order of Polish nuns at a small school here in Melbourne, and the same nuns ran the Polish language school that I attended every week until I was sixteen. So, you see, I'm fluent in Polish, my first language.'

I was conscious of Nadia's commitments in the afternoon, but I was enjoying the conversation and didn't want it to end. I still had many questions.

'Have you been back to Poland?'

'Oh yes. My research focuses on twentieth century Polish literature, so from the time I began my doctorate, I went there once a year. Despite the destruction, a great deal has been preserved, thanks to dedicated patriots who risked their lives to conceal treasured resources. So Colin, while I'm a proud Australian, I am also a citizen of Poland. I love my homeland with a passion.'

'Are you gifted in music like your mother?' I recalled her rich, deep contralto at Borys' funeral.

'I love music, but it wasn't the career I wanted. After I left secondary school, I studied Arts at the same university where I now work. This took me into work as a teacher. In my thirties, I joined the Polish Order of nuns that had taught me in primary school. I was with the Order for ten years, but I found the work unsatisfying, and convent life didn't suit me. I had a burning desire to learn about Polish history and its literature, particularly the literature that arose during the German occupation. I wanted to go to Poland and begin a doctorate, but as a religious sister it was impossible. So I left the Order and taught in state schools for two years to save enough money for my first trip to my homeland. It was the turning point I'd been looking for.'

Ah! Her history was Catholic, just as mine was.

'Did your parents ever go back?'

'Yes, I accompanied them two years after that first return of my own. They still had family and friends there, and we toured the length and breadth of the country. It was very joyful, and I learnt a great deal about my family background. But my parents were pleased to come home to Australia.'

'So since then your life has been in the university?'

'Yes, I have many friends and relatives in Melbourne, but my life has been given to my work. And every now and then there is a moment I'll never forget … like finding Borys Stasiewicz and his poetry in Melbourne. But I'm talking too much. What about you, Colin?'

I told her the bare details of my work on the bench, and something of our family, especially of Mary, but I didn't mention Bernadette's illness. I didn't understand it well enough yet.

All too soon, it was time for her to leave. I felt lighter and happier than I had since this dreadful business began, and I wanted to see Nadia again.

She kissed me lightly on the cheek as she left to walk back to her office. 'I've enjoyed this, Colin. You're a good listener.'

I smiled at that. I was sure my children wouldn't have agreed. 'I've enjoyed it too. May I bring Alison to talk to you?'

Her face lit up in a smile. 'Please do. Call me and we'll make a time.'

Then she was gone, the black cape swirling around her as she strode across the street.

CHAPTER 41
THE AGE
TUESDAY, 10 MAY

Yesterday in the Supreme Court of Victoria, Henry Stanley was sentenced to eighteen years jail for the manslaughter of Borys Staskiewicz, a homeless man who at the time was sleeping in Enterprise Park by the Yarra.

The Presiding Judge, the Honourable Justice Holliman, remarked that although he accepted that the killing was unpremeditated, and taking into account that Stanley had confessed, the viciousness of his attack on a frail, elderly man led him to impose a sentence just below the maximum recommended of twenty years.

Stanley will be eligible for parole in fifteen years.

CHAPTER 42
HARRY (HENRYK STANLEY)
MONDAY, 16 MAY

Well, it's over, the waiting. At least now I know. I'm inside for the best part of twenty years. No point whinging. I'm not scared. I'm a big bloke. I can take care of myself.

It was not too bad in jail. Three meals a day and bit of free time. The worst part was the smell. Blokes stink. And the early lockdown — tea at five and then into the cells for twelve hours. Keep my head down and mind my own business, they told me.

They put me to work in the mornings in the maintenance shed — broken appliances, stripping down and servicing engines. Right up my alley. In the afternoons, there were classes.

Might be a chance to catch up on the schooling I missed when me and the old man lived in the forest camps.

Trent came, that partner of Leo's. It was his day off. Wrote and asked if he could visit. One of the screws read the letter for me. He turned up with the old man's book of poems. Said I could have it now that the case was over. I didn't want it. Couldn't read it, and there was too much to remember anyway — the old man crying over it when he was drunk in those days in the Carlton factory. 'Give it to Allie,' I said.

But why she'd want it I don't know.

So, it's alright. Got my own cell with a bed, basin and toilet, bare walls. I don't have anything else, as it all went up with the house, all of the junk. Too many years of living in junk. Shouldn't have done that to Allie.

Trent said that she was staying with them until they could work something out. Told me that Bernie was still in hospital. She didn't know about me yet. Didn't know what I thought about it all — stuck in jail for years now. Trent asked who I wanted to visit me. You had to put them on a list.

Who would want to visit me? Leo? Why? Bernie never goes anywhere. Allie? No fear. I won't have her going through that. Won't have my lovely Allie in this place. She's got to make her own life now, forget about us. We let her down.

'You could talk to her on the phone,' Trent said.

Said he'd arrange it. Said I could ring her once a week, she missed me, he said.

She must hate me though.

'No,' he said, 'she doesn't, she wants to talk to you. Wants to write you letters too.' She asked Trent to get the permission.

I choked up a bit when he said that. I didn't deserve her. She was the one good thing in my life, but I didn't want her in this rough place.

Okay, I'll call her every Saturday in the morning. That's when you can line up for the phone, and she's got that job on a Sunday. When she's eighteen, she might come. We'll see.

CHAPTER 43
LEO BRENNAN
MONDAY, 16 MAY

No! Not this. Not now. The thing I've dreamed of, waited for, prayed for even, if my vague pleas out to the universe can be called 'prayer'.

I was up early this morning to drop Alison at the pool and get a run on my emails before bookings took over.

I was constantly sending photos to magazines, in the hope of attracting a commission, and now, here it was. I'd almost forgotten that I had entered a competition in *Outback Roads* some months ago. It was a new magazine, aimed at caravanners, campers and four-wheel drivers, and it specialised in 'off the grid' features about tiny outback towns and rural industry. It used wonderful images, and I didn't think that I could win, but I put my photo in anyway. I'd taken it the year before when Trent and I did a short road trip into outback New South Wales. We stayed at a sheep station that was managed by an ex-cop mate of Trent's, and we were there for the shearing.

The photo showed a mob of sheep being mustered into the holding yards in front of the shed. It was wall-to-wall thick wool, and looking at the image you could almost smell the dust, feel the flies on your face and hear the frightened braying of the sheep. But the photo wasn't really about the sheep. The focus was the dog, a red kelpie. A moment before, he'd been mustering the sheep, jumping on their backs, and from one sheep to the next, he was bothering them, moving them forward, doing his job.

From the side of the yard, I called to him, 'Red dog!'

He stopped for a split second, looked at me and into the camera from his platform on the back of a huge sheep, and his face split in a grin of pure dog happiness. I had the shot in an instant, and he was back to his work, everywhere at once working the sheep. It was an image in time, so Australian, so of the bush and the outback, so joyful.

I'd won the competition!

You know that feeling when something happens that you didn't dare hope for, something so good, so unreal, that you'll remember the moment forever. Something you have to keep reminding yourself is actually real.

The prize was $2000 and a commission for a photo essay on remote outback pubs, twenty images in all accompanied by notes for the editor to work into text. Basic expenses would be covered, and I'd be paid a retainer and for each image when it was published. I was to submit the work in early May the following year.

It was a dream, a miracle, but I couldn't do it. It would mean at least three months away. I had events booked for the rest of the year, and I wouldn't let clients down, so I couldn't plan the trip until next year. I could do it between January and April, but there was one problem with that …

Alison.

She was starting Year Twelve next year, and she had nowhere else to live. Trent's hours were too unpredictable to rely on him being there for her. I'd have to turn it down.

ALL DAY I kept coming back to the commission, worrying at it like a broken tooth. By the evening, the euphoria of winning had worn away. I was tired and depressed, but resolute that I would have to turn down the opportunity.

Then I told Trent.

We couldn't keep anything from each other. There was nowhere to hide in our relationship, and by the time he'd been home for an hour, he knew everything, including my conviction that I had to refuse the prize.

Trent was a more lateral thinker than me; perhaps that was why he was such a good detective. He saw things from many angles, while I, often emotional and tragic, settled early for the most obvious result.

'It's brilliant, Leo, wonderful,' he said, holding me tight in our tiny kitchen as I chapped vegetables for dinner.

'I can't accept it.' I was stubborn now in my resolution that Alison's care and safety had to be my priority.

Trent took the sharp knife from my hands. 'Leave the damn vegetables. Come and sit down and let's look at this together.'

So we did, me bleating about it being the wrong time, and the fact that there would be later, more convenient commissions. Trent arguing that there were other options for Alison, and then me countering.

'What options? Her father's in jail and her mother is incapable of being a parent to her, even if she does leave hospital in the near future.'

Trent then brought up the thought that was floating between us. 'The Judge?'

'He's too old?'

'He's fit and healthy. What does he do all day at that house in Golden Beach anyway? Fishing? Pottering around? He's not ready to give up yet.'

Then Trent delivered the line he knew would nail it. 'I'll take Long Service Leave. I'll come with you. We'll hire a campervan and be grey nomads for three months.'

I looked at him, the thick beard, the kind eyes, the scruffy jumper and runners, the love in his face. 'Would you?'

'Of course.' His face was gleeful.

'But Alison?' I was still not convinced.

'Look, talk to the Judge. Tell him about this opportunity. See how he feels about making a home for Alison while she does Year Twelve.'

'It will be longer than that. We can't have her going off alone to some university college when she finishes school.' I was adamant about that.

'As I said, talk to the Judge.'

His common sense and balance finally got through to me as it always did. 'Okay, it can't hurt to try.'

'Exactly.' He went back to the kitchen, took up the knife and returned to the vegetables.

CHAPTER 44
ALISON BRENNAN
TUESDAY, 24 MAY

My grandfather's poems. I have the book here on Grandma's desk in my room at Uncle Leo's house.

Trent told me that he'd asked Dad if he wanted the book, but Dad said no, to give it to me.

'The book is very rare and precious,' Trent said.

There were only about thirty copies printed. I couldn't read the poems because they were all in Polish, but it was surreal to hold them in my hands, knowing that the book had survived the war, the concentration camps, and my grandfather's life when he came to Australia. It must have been so precious to him. The book was very old and dilapidated. If Dad was here, I'd ask him to help me mend it, but he's not here. I'd have to mend it myself.

Grandpa said we'd go together to see Professor Godlewski. She was that Polish woman who sang the prayer at my grandfather's funeral. He said that she'd translate the poems for me.

Trent said that Dad was okay. I could write to him, and Dad was going to ring me every week.

CHAPTER 45

LEO BRENNAN

SATURDAY, 28 MAY

Alison and I had visited Bernie three times now, and each time there was the same passive resistance. She was either playing cards, or pretending to read a magazine. There was no conversation, but you could tell that she was keenly aware of us by the slight tremor in her hand, and the way she snatched a glance at us when she thought we weren't watching.

It was hard on Alison. She believed she was still being punished for going to the Judge's house at Easter. It was a lot for her to carry — she was just a kid, but she sat there and tried to talk to her mother, telling her about school and her friend Rosa. Anything to fill the silence.

Today the Judge came with me. The doctor had given reserved permission. 'He must leave immediately if she becomes distressed,' we were warned.

The passivity Bernie had shown to me and Alison was so unlike distress that I thought there'd be no problem, although I was aware of the need for caution. The relationship between the Judge and Bernie had never been close, disappointment on his side, fear and subservience on hers.

I was nervous when I entered her room. The Judge was

just a little behind me. Bernie sat in the same seat by the window, dressed neatly in some of the clothes Alison and I had bought for her. She was knitting today, something I hadn't seen her do for years. She'd given up all her hobbies when Mum died, but Bernie's knitting, embroidery and crocheting were once exquisite. For a few years she exhibited some of her work at the Melbourne Show. Today it was a thin strip of plain knitting, like a scarf for a doll, in a pale-blue wool.

She looked up when I entered, and then back down at her needles again, and then up again when the Judge greeted her.

'Hello Bernadette.'

Although I'd never seen a volcano erupting, it was the only thing to which I could liken what happened next.

The blood drained from her face, her chair jerked back as she thrust herself up, the knitting fell to the floor. She lunged at the Judge, yelling, spitting saliva in his face, bombarding him with slaps to his chest, pushing him away. 'No, no, get out, don't come here,' she screamed.

The Judge tried to fend her off. 'Settle down, Bernadette. Sit down, please dear.'

'I won't sit down … I won't … I won't do anything you say.' Her ineffectual slaps to his chest continued.

The Judge fended her off gently. 'What's wrong, Bernadette? Tell me.'

'Alright, I will tell you, I'll tell you now … should have years ago … your fault … horrible man, came to my room, pulled my nightgown off, *raped me*.' She screamed the last two words at the top of her lungs, her face blue with the effort. Her eyes were wild, crazy. 'That rapist,' she screamed, 'in our house, in Mummy's house.'

'Rapist?' the Judge repeated, still shielding himself from her blows. 'What rapist? You're imagining things, Bernadette.'

For one appalling moment I thought she was accusing the Judge of raping her.

Suddenly her voice was very clam and clear. She stopped

beating at his chest and stood in front of him. Despite her weight, she seemed very small before the Judge's height.

'It's time I told you.' She was breathing heavily and sweating. 'That pig that was always in our house. The four of you eating and drinking downstairs. He came to my room.'

'Who on earth are you talking about?'

'The red-faced man, always drunk, he came upstairs, came into my room.' Then she began to shake with loud sobs. 'No … no … no.' She threw herself to the floor on her knees then curled into a ball and rocked herself, saying over and over, 'He raped me. He came to my room, his hand was at my throat, and he pushed my head up to the bedhead and forced me. I tried to scream but he covered my mouth. I bit him, and he swore at me, but he wouldn't stop. He said never to tell, that no one would believe me.'

The Judge stood immobile. 'Who on earth?'

I watched as something crossed over his face, some memory.

'Good God, you can't mean Jack Constable.'

She rose again to her feet and confronted the Judge, calm now. 'Yes, your friend, Jack Constable, the red-faced pig.'

She and the Judge stood staring at each other for what seemed like long minutes but must only have been a few seconds.

I went to her, took her hands and guided her back to her chair by the window, leaving the Judge standing, stunned. 'Bernie, why didn't you say something?'

'He said not to. He threatened me.' She was quieter now. 'I was so scared. I didn't really understand what had happened.'

She let me hold her then. 'I'm so sorry, Bernie, so very sorry. Did Mum know?'

She wouldn't look at the Judge but said firmly to me, 'Not then … later…Tell him to go. I never want to see him again. He's a monster. He's never cared about me.'

The Judge was pale and shaken, but Bernie was the important one for now. I asked him, gently, to wait for me in the visitor's room.

At last she was calm. She picked up her knitting and began working on it again. 'Go now, Leo, I'm okay.'

It was the first time she'd used my name since that horrible night when Alison found her huddled in her bed.

I kissed her cheek. 'I'm glad you told us, Bernie. I'm so sorry for what you had to go through.'

The Judge looked every moment of his eighty or so years when I met him in the visitor's room — slouched, drawn, all the authority punched out of him.

CHAPTER 46

BERNADETTE BRENNAN

SATURDAY, 28 MAY

WHEN LEO LEFT I RAN TO THE TOILET AND VOMITED, kneeling on the cold floor. Everything came up until there was nothing but water. I sat there for a long time, my eyes and nose running and my throat aching. I remembered the winey, boozy smell of him, the way his hands clutched at me, and the disgusting noises he made, the feeling that I was going to suffocate … and the pain and the blood. Couldn't stop shaking.

I cried and cried until there were no tears left … not for now. I cried for the dead baby, how Mummy baptised him and took him away wrapped in a towel. I didn't tell them about that.

Then the nurse came and helped me up, wiped my face and tucked me up in bed like a child.

CHAPTER 47

COLIN BRENNAN

SATURDAY, 28 MAY

If only I could pretend that she had imagined it, put it down to her mental illness. Or that she made the story up to punish me for my emotional neglect, or even that the smug little doctor put the accusation into her head.

But in my moments of clarity, I knew that none of that would wash. Jack Constable was a lecher. There were plenty of sleazy stories, and Bernadette wouldn't have been the first innocent young woman he preyed upon.

But when I faced the story's truth, I was left with very little, just a self-important man who let a rapist roam his house unchecked; a man who didn't protect his daughter; a man who let a criminal into his home over and over again; a man who cared more for his standing in the judicial community than for his relationship with his child.

Shame is what I'm left with. I'm left with just Colin Brennan, a pathetic failure as a man and a father.

Yes, I was ashamed of myself and mortified that this happened, angry that I failed the most important test of all. But when I thought of Constable, when his big, red face came into my mind, I wanted to beat it to the consistency of minced meat. I wanted to urinate on his grave. I wanted to dig up his bones and rotting flesh and spread them across the city.

There was no redress — the man was dead.

Perhaps Bernadette could sue his estate, but it was only her word. They'd portray her as delusional, a psychiatric patient fabricating lies about a respected member of the Melbourne judiciary. She'd have to testify and there'd be a panic attack, even if she agreed to do it. We couldn't put her through it. So that was it. There were no witnesses and the only person who could corroborate her claim was Mary, also deceased.

Sylvia was still alive. She'd shout and bluster and accuse Bernadette of lying, accuse me of jealously trying to besmirch the reputation of her noble husband, but she would have heard the rumours, just like everyone else. There might be some small satisfaction in confronting her.

I didn't know where to go to from here. I was tired of the stuffy Club, the memory of Constable and his like all around me. I wanted to go home to Golden Beach, but something had to be decided about Alison.

Then there was Bernadette. As Leo would say: 'It's not about you, Dad.'

I was not used to thinking about her as a real person, trying to imagine her feelings. She said that I never cared about her. She was probably right. Mostly, she was an annoyance.

Good God, how I've behaved!

CHAPTER 48
LEO BRENNAN
SATURDAY, 28 MAY

FOR THE FIRST TIME EVER I FELT SORRY FOR THE OLD BOY. HE was trembling as I helped him into the car, and I had to wait as he fumbled with his seatbelt.

'Are you okay, Dad,' I asked, as I pulled out into the traffic.

'I will be, I suppose,' he said.

We didn't talk as we drove into the city. Bernie's story was horrible and heavy between us.

When I pulled up outside his Club, it was still the middle of the afternoon. As I helped him out of the car he seemed old and frail. It struck me that I was treating him like a geriatric relative. He must have hated it.

'Look Dad,' I said, 'there's obviously a lot we need to talk about. Can you get some rest this afternoon? I'd like to come back and have dinner with you this evening. Sort some things out.'

He nodded.

'See you here at six?'

'Yes, Leo, good.' He shook my hand then, and I watched as he walked slowly through the heavy doors.

. . .

I HATED THE CLUB — stuffy armchairs, obsequious waiters, the trappings of old money, inflated old men with the occasional token female guest. It wasn't my scene, but it was Dad's turf and I wanted him to be comfortable.

He waited in the lounge, at a corner table, private behind a Japanese-themed screen. We both ordered beer.

'How are you, Dad?' I asked, shaking his hand.

He was trembling slightly and his eyes were watery. 'I've been better.'

I began cautiously. 'Did you know anything of what Bernie told us this afternoon?'

'No, of course not. It rocked me to the core. I knew nothing, nothing.'

'But she said Mum knew. Later at least.'

'That doesn't surprise me. Your mother and Bernadette were very close. Bernadette told her everything. The rape …' he grimaced as he said the word, 'was probably what set off her first breakdown. I wish your mother had told me, but that was her way of course.'

'What, to protect you?' That would be typical of Mum.

'Yes, perhaps to protect me, but maybe it was just easier the less I knew. Unfortunately I used to make a fuss.'

'But this was something to make a fuss about. He should have been charged.'

'And so he would have been, had I known.' He paused. 'You know, I can't get out of my head that blundering fool having the nerve … you don't expect a guest in your home to go prowling around and rape your daughter.'

I let him talk. He was full of shame and anger, and he blamed himself. But he was also bewildered. How could it have happened when he and Mum, not to mention the Constable's wife, were sitting downstairs? Why didn't Bernie tell them right away?

'Dad, you hear it all the time. Rapists often terrify their victims into saying nothing. Tell them it was their fault, that no one will believe them; that their reputation will be shot, that sort of thing. You must know this from your time on the bench.'

'Yes, but you don't apply what you experience on the bench to your own family … How can I help her, Leo? I have almost no connection with her and she seems to hate me.'

'Yes, she's afraid of you. Feels she hasn't lived up to expectations. But Dad, simple kindness is quite an easy thing. It might be the place to start.'

We were called to dinner then, but we continued to talk with an ease I hadn't experienced with him before. He was humbled and bewildered, and I could see that he was turning Bernie's story over and over in his mind.

But there was something else, and I had to mention it. 'Dad, we need to make a decision about Alison.'

'Yes, yes,' he said distracted.

'Alison needs a secure and permanent home. She'll be in Year Twelve next year and she needs space to study.'

'Of course.'

I decided I'd take this gradually. 'The room she's using was my office where I kept my equipment, met clients and did my accounts. It wasn't even adequate for that. Since Alison's been there, I have had to store equipment wherever I can find a space, and meeting clients is difficult. The only space we have is the living area, and if Trent and Alison are both home, it's hopeless.'

'Yes,' he said. 'It's a tiny house. I can see the problem.'

He was drifting again, no doubt back to the scene at the hospital. I had to keep him on track. 'There's another thing, Dad.'

I told him about the prize I'd won, and the prospect of a three-month commission in the outback early in the following year. I had his attention now. I thought that he'd disparage the idea, knowing that he had little respect for my profession, but he stared at me as if taking it in, and then he smiled, and to my surprise and pleasure, he reached across to shake my hand.

'Congratulations, Leo. What an opportunity. Your first real commission, eh?'

'Yes, but there's Alison.' I wanted him to come to the solution himself, but he put it back to me.

'What do you propose?'

'Alison coming to us was always only an interim measure, a response to an emergency. I was determined to get her out of that house, but I don't think our place is the permanent solution. And now this has come up. I can't go and leave her for three months.'

'I do see the difficulty.'

'Dad, what about you? You and Alison are close.'

'Yes, we are now, thank God. I love the dear child.' He smiled again.

Was this the Judge speaking? *Love* wasn't a word I often heard from him.

Then he said, 'What are you getting at, Leo?'

Was he being deliberately obtuse or was this all too much after the revelations of the afternoon? So I just came out and asked, 'Would it work for Alison to live with you?'

'What, at Golden Beach?' He looked genuinely surprised.

'No, of course not. She has to go to school. But won't there be an insurance payout on the Clifton Hill house?'

Did I need to spell it out for him?

'Yes, a decent amount, my accountant tells me. And when the rubble's cleared, I'll sell the block.'

'Well? Join the dots, Dad. A small house or apartment here in Melbourne for you and Alison. Somewhere close to her school. Somewhere she can have friends. Golden Beach will always be there to go back to.' I watched him take the idea in — turn over its possibilities.

He shrugged. 'I'm an old man, Leo. I'm not much fun for a teenage girl.'

'Dad, Alison's no ordinary teenager. She's lived in dirt and chaos most of her life and she's still turned out warm-hearted and kind … and very independent.'

'Yes, she's a wonderful girl. Like your mother.'

'She didn't descend into the mess of that house, but she needs somewhere clean, secure and orderly now, somewhere she can study, where she has privacy and a routine, somewhere she feels wanted. Somewhere she can finish her VCE. She needs an adult in her life. Despite everything, she still loves her parents and doesn't blame them for anything. But we can't expect her to take responsibility for her mother again. She was virtually Bernie's unpaid carer, and it's too much. Anyway, Bernie could be in hospital for months, we don't know what her future is. Alison has the right to her own life … and Dad, she loves you.'

'I know.'

We were both silent while he considered the idea.

He then said, 'Let's talk about it a bit more. Where would you think?'

'Anywhere she can get a tram or walk to school.'

'I like the idea, but we need to see what Alison thinks. What's happening tomorrow?' Suddenly he had more energy.

'She's working, and then Trent or I usually take her to visit Bernie for an hour or so. She'll be home by six. Come over and have something to eat with us and we'll put the idea to her.'

He agreed.

Thank God that's over, I thought. *This might be the beginning of something good for all of us.*

There were more shocks to come, but for tonight the Judge had something to plan for.

CHAPTER 49

ALISON BRENNAN

SUNDAY, 29 MAY

It's been weeks since I slept in that house. I know it's burned down now, but I still have nightmares about it. I dream that I'm back in my room, and it's the middle of the night, and there's a rat biting my foot.

In another dream, something really horrible, alive, is trying to get out of the fridge. Other times, I'm trying to clean, but the more rubbish I pick up, the more the piles grow, and I'm scratching and scratching because there are tiny fleas crawling all over me.

Then I wake up sweating and shouting and remember that I'm at Leo's house. I'm safe; it was only a dream. But the feeling of relief is followed by wide-awake worrying. Everything crowds into my mind together. What will happen to Mum? Will she ever get well? Is Dad safe in jail? Where am I going to live?

Mrs Goodall told me about visualisation, how visualising certain 'happy' things could help you to be calm, and so when I was wide-awake and worrying in the early hours of the morning, I had a special visualisation I did.

I imagined my perfect home. It was small, but not cramped, just big enough for me. It was painted pure, clean white. There were white tiles in the kitchen and bathroom, and shiny wood floors with bright mats. There was no piece of hair or fluff or dust on any of them. The benches in the kitchen and bathroom were a rich blue. The whole house was spotlessly clean and there was nothing in it that wasn't necessary.

There was space in the cupboards for everything to be put away, and all the benchtops and surfaces were clear. There were no dusty ornaments, congealing soap or tatty cushions and doilies. The fridge held only clean, fresh food, and only as much as I needed. My bed was thick, with white, cotton sheets and a white quilt. There was a bookcase with all the books I loved. Everything smelt very faintly of sandalwood, the same oil Mrs Goodall liked to burn in her office.

After a while of imagining my perfect home, I fell asleep again.

TODAY WAS SUNDAY. I worked at Hungry Jacks, and then Trent drove me to the hospital to see Mum. He waited outside, and I bought flowers for her at the little shop in the lobby. When I had taken some flowers to her on Mother's Day, her face had lit up, so I decided to take some every visit.

Mum was sitting in the same chair by the window, but today she was knitting. I'd never seen her knit before, and I didn't even know she knew how to, or how she learnt to knit. It was a thin strip, blue, almost long enough to tie around my waist. Mum actually spoke to me this time.

'Hello, dear,' she said.

She didn't say my name. Did she know who I was, I wondered? 'Mum, it's me, Alison.'

'Yes, I know,' she said, still knitting.

So I talked about school, and about Leo and Trent. I didn't mention Grandpa. I asked her what she was making and who it was for. She didn't really answer me, just made vague little noises, but she smiled once or twice when I told her funny stories about school. She smiled again while I arranged the flowers in a vase.

After an hour I kissed her goodbye and told her I'd come again next Sunday. Just as I was leaving, I thought of something. 'Mum, would you teach me how to knit?'

She met my eyes then, and nodded her head, just slightly.

Next time I'd bring wool and knitting needles.

WHEN WE GOT BACK to Leo's house, Grandpa was there. There was a funny feeling. Something was happening, as if they'd been talking about me.

When we sat down to eat, Leo said, 'Allie, there's something your grandpa and I want to discuss with you.'

'Yes? What it is?' I asked. I pretended not to be concerned, to give my attention to the food, but I was listening carefully.

'It's been a terrible time for you. I know how worried you must be about your parents. I suppose you're also worried about where you're going to live.'

I didn't want Leo to think I was ungrateful, but I did worry. There wasn't enough room for the three of us in this tiny house. Also, Mum would need somewhere to live when she came out of hospital, but I didn't think I could look after Mum without Dad there. I'd have to leave school. All of this was going through my mind.

Leo told me then about his prize and his commission for an outback photography trip early next year. He'd be away for three months, and he was hoping Trent could go with him. I was excited for him, but more worried than ever. Where would I go? And what about Mum?

Then Grandpa told us his idea.

'So,' he said, 'I was thinking that I'd like to buy an apartment close to your school, where you and I could live at least until you've finished Year Twelve.'

I wondered if I'd heard him correctly. 'What about Golden Beach?'

'We can go there for holidays.'

'But what about Mum? When she comes out of hospital?'

'We don't know what may be best for your mum in the future, Alison. We have to be guided by her doctor. But we'll make sure there's a room there for her when she needs it.'

Uncle Leo was staring at him. Maybe they hadn't talked about that part.

I put my head down to hide my face, but the tears rolled down and soaked into the tablecloth. I was so tired and so sick of being worried.

'Why, dear girl,' Grandpa said, 'I didn't mean to upset you. If you prefer to stay here with Leo and Trent, we can arrange something.'

I stood, went to the back of Grandpa's chair and put my arms around his neck. I remembered Golden Beach and how quiet and restful it was to live with him, how we ate good food and how we both worked peacefully in the evenings.

'Grandpa, it's perfect. Just perfect. I'm crying because I'm relieved and happy.'

He just patted my hand, and said, 'It's time you were happy.'

So we talked about where we might begin looking, and pulled up some internet sites that advertised apartments for sale, close to the city on a tram line. The school holidays were coming soon and Grandpa and I would go house hunting,

I didn't have bad dreams that night, and I didn't have to use my visualisation.

CHAPTER 50
COLIN BRENNAN
FRIDAY, 3 JUNE

THREE DAYS AFTER BERNADETTE REVEALED THAT SHE HAD BEEN raped by Jack Constable, Dr Sarah Soliman called me to say that Bernadette had requested a family conference with Leo and me.

'Is this usual?' I asked.

'It's not unusual. Sometimes bringing the family in at crucial times in a person's therapy can be beneficial.'

'Very well.'

What now? I thought. I was beginning to feel like one of those puppets at a sideshow where you threw a ball to knock it down and it sprang up again, leering at you. I didn't know how many more knocks I could take. There would be no good news in this 'conference', I was sure. Leo was free the following Friday morning, so we made it for ten o'clock.

WE WERE SHOWN into a sitting room, pleasant enough, with flowers and sun coming through the window, although the day was cold. Thank God it wasn't the stuffy little visitor's room where Sarah Soliman had lectured me the last time I was here.

Bernadette looked exhausted. She had dark circles under her eyes, as if she hadn't slept, but her demeanour was different somehow. She met my eyes when we came into the room. 'Hello Daddy, hello Leo,' she said in that high, childlike voice.

There was none of the hostility with which she'd greeted me last Sunday.

We sat then, but I couldn't escape the same impression that I was on trial for some unconscious transgression.

Dr Soliman began, 'Thank you for coming, Colin and Leo. Incidentally, may I use first names?'

We both nodded.

'And please call me Sarah. Bernadette is taking an important step today, and I'm here to support her, not to direct the conference in any way. The conversation is between you three. Is that understood?'

Again, we nodded.

'Last Saturday, Bernadette revealed to you details of the crime that was committed against her when she was a young woman of twenty-one.'

'Yes,' I said, 'that she was raped in our home by someone I thought I could trust.'

'Don't blame yourself, Colin. You had no knowledge of it, and as you say you trusted this person, who I understand is dead now. However, Bernadette has asked me to be here because there's another aspect of the crime that she wants out in the open. Are you ready, Bernadette?'

'Yes.' Bernadette sat straight in her chair, her hands joined in her lap. They were trembling. She spoke as if she'd rehearsed the words many times. 'When it happened, it was just after my twenty-first birthday. Do you remember, Daddy, that you and Mummy gave me those lovely pearls?'

Yes, I remembered. Mary had ordered them through a jeweller in Broome. I felt sure Bernadette would lose them.

'Anyway, that's not important,' she said. 'When he came to

my room and did that to me, I really didn't understand what was happening. I knew it was wrong and it felt dirty, but I didn't know what it was. I was a very silly, inexperienced girl, and I'd been so sheltered.' She paused.

Leo and I sat waiting.

'Okay, Bernadette?' the doctor asked.

Bernadette took a deep breath and sipped from the glass of water on the table before her. 'Thank you, Sarah, I'm fine.' She paused slightly, before continuing, 'So as you know, I was very innocent. He said not to tell anyone and I didn't, not even Mummy … but … but nine months later there was a baby.'

No! I could feel my stomach sink to the floor and my heart rate increase. *Not that, please.*

Bernadette kept talking in that rehearsed way. 'I had no idea I was pregnant. No idea at all. I could see that I was getting bigger, but I've always been large so I thought nothing of it. I've never cared about my appearance. I ate whatever I wanted and I never did any exercise, so it stood to reason that I'd gain weight. Really, when I think back, I knew so little about my body.'

So much for Catholic education and its prurience about sex education, I thought. *Those nuns have a lot to answer for.*

'Then one night I began to have what I now know were contractions. They went for hours. Indigestion, I thought, something bad that I ate, perhaps. But I must have called out because Mummy came.' Bernadette's mouth twitched. She was trying hard not to break down. 'Mummy delivered the baby. It was dead — blue, purplish.'

Sarah stretched out her hand to cover Bernadette's.

'It's okay, Sarah, I'm not going to cry.'

The silence in the room was a thick cloud, palpable.

'What happened to the child, dear?' I asked softly.

Then she did cry, gasping for breath so we had to strain to

understand. 'Mummy … Mummy took it. She baptised it so it wouldn't go to Limbo. Then she took it away.'

What a nonsensical notion 'Limbo' always was, discredited now of course. My mind kept working, even as I tried to absorb the dreadful story.

'Took it where, Bernie?' Leo asked.

'I don't know. She said everything would be alright. She cleaned me, gave me a pill and told me to sleep. She said we wouldn't tell anyone. She told me to stay in bed. And I did, for weeks. It was just after that that I went into hospital, and then I began seeing Dr Werstein.'

'Did she ask you who it was, the father I mean?' Leo asked.

'Yes, but I didn't tell.'

So Constable — that putrid excuse for a human being — got away with it. I wished I'd known. I'd have had him in court in five minutes. We could have taken DNA samples. Could have put him in jail. Honestly, I didn't know if I could take anymore of this.

Bernadette's story rang true for me in every detail. It would be just like Mary to do what was necessary, dispose of the baby's body, care for Bernadette, keep the whole thing from me, the self-righteous Judge whom, she was sure, would see it as one more disruption to his life by his foolish daughter. Mary baptising the baby was so typical of her that I almost wept.

I wished desperately that she'd told me. I wished she'd given me the chance to be compassionate, to be a father, to get some justice for Bernadette. I swallowed my outrage. As Leo would say, this wasn't about me. 'What do you want to do about it, Bernadette?' I asked. 'Do you want us to go to his family? Demand reparation? There's some possibility that we could sue his estate.'

She looked terrified. 'No, Daddy, no … no … I just wanted you and Leo to know, so you'd understand … you know, my problems, why I have no confidence … you know, scared to leave the house. I just wanted you to know, that's all.'

'You've been very brave, Bernie.' Leo went to her chair and knelt before it, taking her hands. 'I will do anything … anything to help you get stronger.'

Bernadette patted his hand in an absent way. She seemed relieved that the story had been told.

'Where to from here?' I asked Dr Soliman.

'That's up to Bernadette. Telling you about the situation has been a breakthrough for her, and she's been very brave. But she knows that it's only one step. There is still a long way to go. She must do the work. I'm just here for support and guidance.'

There's still so much poor Bernadette doesn't know, I thought … about Harry, his crime, the torching of the house, his incarceration … but now certainly wasn't the time to tell her.

I thanked Dr Soliman, and on an impulse I stood and held out my arms to Bernadette. I couldn't remember when I had last hugged her. A very long time, I was sure. I expected her to refuse my embrace, but she came into my arms and I held her briefly.

'I am so sorry, darling,' I said.

'Yes, Daddy.' She patted my back as if it was she comforting me.

CHAPTER 51

COLIN BRENNAN

SUNDAY, 5 JUNE

THERE WAS A 'FOR SALE' SIGN ON THE FENCE BY THE GATE. I remembered the house. It was a particularly lovely two-storey Federation home in South Yarra. The leadlight windows were original, and the small veranda where I stood was shaded by a red-flowering gum. The north-facing formal garden was meticulously kept. The doorbell was answered by a man in his thirties wearing an apron over blue jeans and a white T-shirt. The son, I realised. I'd never met him. As I recalled, he was their only child.

'Hello, I was hoping to see Sylvia.'

He looked at me with suspicion. 'Yes, that's my mother. What's it about?'

'Oh, sorry.' I extended my hand. 'I'm Colin Brennan, an old friend of your parents. I couldn't get to your father's funeral, so I wanted to pay my respects to your mother.'

He relaxed then and shook my hand. 'Judge Brennan. We haven't met, but of course I knew of you when I was growing up. Mum's here, but I'm not sure how well she is this morning.'

He led me through a wide, tiled entrance to an elegant sitting room. Sylvia sat in a floral covered armchair in front of a glowing log fire. She didn't look up when we entered, but she patted and murmured to a small dog on her lap, a prissily groomed poodle, which yapped sharply at me.

'Mum,' David said. 'Judge Brennan is here to see you.'

An old woman, she looked up slowly, watery eyes struggling to focus. Then a tremulous smile crossed her face. 'There you are darling Jack, you're home. Puddles and I have been waiting for you.' She stroked the ear of the silly dog. Then turning to David, she said, 'Bring my husband a drink please, then we'll have dinner in an hour.'

I looked at my watch. It was ten in the morning.

'Now, sit down Jack dear, and tell me about work. How's the Renton trial going?'

The Renton trial was a famous one that Constable had presided over. A man killed his wife and four children and staged it as a murder-suicide. It had ended twenty years before with the conviction of Renton and his lover.

David raised his eyebrows at me. 'Dementia,' he whispered. 'Today's a bad day, I'm afraid. She thinks I'm the cook.'

'I'll bring you a cup of tea and a biscuit, Mum. What about you, Judge Brennan?'

'Call me Colin, please. Just a cup of black coffee.'

Although Sylvia was shrunken with age, there was still something of the imperious, bossy socialite in her manner. 'Jack, I can't get any work out of this new woman.' There followed five minutes or so of domestic troubles ranging from inadequate dinner menus to the gardener bringing dirt into the lobby.

'Sylvia, it's Colin Brennan. Remember you were friends with my wife, Mary?'

For a moment the cloud seemed to clear, and then it settled again. 'Oh, Mary Brennan. Yes, I ran into her in Toorak Road yesterday. I must invite her for lunch, dear Mary. But one is so busy.'

Through my hazy memories of Mary's funeral, I recalled that Jack and Sylvia had been there — Jack self-important in his morning suit, and Sylvia in designer black.

David brought in the tea and coffee, and we sat in silence as Sylvia caressed the hostile little dog.

'How's your health, Sylvia?' I asked, hoping she might recognise me just for a moment. 'Are you well?'

'Why, Jack,' she said, 'you know I'm well, but it's sweet of you to be concerned. Now, don't forget we've got that tennis party with the deputy Premier at the weekend. I hope you're going to be free. It's so embarrassing when you make excuses.'

It was fruitless. I stayed as long as was decent, and then I rose to leave.

'Where are you going, Jack? You know we've got guests for dinner.'

I bent and kissed her. 'Just back to chambers for an hour or so, dear, then I'll be here to pour the drinks.'

I followed David to the door.

'Sorry you had to see her like that,' he said.

'Yes, it's sad isn't it? Are you her carer?'

'Just for now. She's moving to a nursing home next week where she'll get the constant care she needs. She's going downhill rapidly, as you saw. Then I have to pack up the house.'

'I see you're selling it. It's a magnificent property.'

'Yes, it's under offer. Not that there'll be much left after I've invested money for Mum's care and paid off sundry debts.' He looked angry, suddenly. 'I'm afraid Dad owed a lot to various "creditors", shall we call them.'

'Banks?'

'If only! No, gambling debts to some really shady outfits. There was an irresponsible side to the old man that Mum and I are still paying for.'

'I'm sorry for that, David. I had no idea.'

'Most people didn't. Mum worked very hard to keep up appearances.'

So that was it. 'Karma,' Leo would say. The story I had come to tell Sylvia would remain with me. I wouldn't inflict it on this innocent man, Constable's son.

I shook his hand with what I hoped was warmth. 'I wish you and your mother well, David.'

I SAT in my car outside the house, the key not fully turned in the ignition. A voice on Radio National discussed a film review with an actor I'd never heard of. What did any of it matter? Sylvia slumped in that armchair, living in the past. That's what happened to the bright, surging spark of life that propelled us into the world; the body became a shell and the mind slowly leaked away.

It would happen to me soon enough.

Unbidden memories of Bernadette as a child came up to meet me. Playing in the shallows at Sorrento, a T-shirt and hat protecting her fair skin. Running to me when I came in the door from work, my hug and greeting never warm enough. Sticky little fingers on my best suit, and Mary hurrying to pull her away. Taking tea with her dolls in the garden, chattering to them. Those golden moments gone. The concerts and Speech nights I rarely found time to attend. The years of school uniforms, books and sport, her hopes for my approval gradually vanishing.

Over the years, I must have become just a frequent, rather frightening visitor to her. It was always Mary. 'Mummy' she would call. I couldn't remember when she stopped calling to me, stopped expecting anything of me.

Then the decline into cloying dependence on her mother and the first signs of agoraphobia … and … Jack Constable.

I let that happen.

And Sylvia.

At the end of life, we became children again.

'WHAT A TRULY SAD STORY,' Nadia said when I told her later that afternoon when we met up.

After the disastrous visit with Sylvia, I had nowhere to go. I couldn't face Leo, and by now I was finding the Club suffocating. I had called her from my car, waiting for the slump in my gut if she told me she was busy. But no, we met in the Botanical Gardens, since I was in South Yarra. It had been years since Nadia had been there, so it was a pleasant way to spend a Sunday afternoon.

We walked the green corridors of the gardens, along the Australian Forest Walk, and towards the Herbarium, pausing to watch toddlers playing in the Children's Garden. We bought picnic food at the café and walked along the Hopetoun Lawn and around the lake.

I told her everything about the various stages of Bernadette's illness, her relationship with Harry, Alison's birth, her hoarding, and this latest dreadful revelation of the crime committed against her by Jack Constable and the stillborn infant. I poured it all out, no longer caring for my dignity or bothering to pretend that I was above it all.

By the time we found a seat in the sun at Picnic Point, Nadia knew more about my family and my self-doubt than I had ever confided to anyone.

'I feel like a criminal,' I told her. 'I've let my children down. I should have been a better father. I don't know how to make it up to Bernadette.'

'We're all inadequate, Colin,' she said. 'We all let others and ourselves down. You have to stop whipping yourself about it all. I'm a believer in the practical. You can't change the past but you can choose the kind and good thing in the present.'

'That's what Leo says. Start with an act of kindness and multiply it. If you don't *feel* love, act as if you do.'

'I think I'd like Leo,' she said.

The conversation moved on. Nadia was applying for funding to establish a Centre for Polish Studies at the university. She outlined her hopes for it, as well as her frustration with the endless paperwork. She asked me again about Stasiewicz's book of poems, and when I told her that Alison had it she seemed pleased.

'I wonder if she'd lend it to me. I'd love to show it to some of my students, and even to begin translating some of the work.'

'You'll need to ask her. I'll bring her to meet you.'

As we strolled I described my home at Golden Beach, and my intention to purchase an apartment for Alison and me, to give her a home until she finished school. Depending on Bernadette's health, it might also become a home for her. I would then transfer the title to Alison when she turned eighteen.

As we explored the Fern Garden, Nadia took my arm, smiling at me. At that moment my failings seemed to matter a little less. Neither of us were young, but there was time yet, and perhaps more sweet moments like this to come — or so I hoped.

CHAPTER 52

ALISON BRENNAN

SUNDAY, 5 JUNE

My hair smelled of grease from the Hungry Jacks' kitchen, but it didn't matter. Mum and I were knitting squares.

'We must have the same size needle,' she said. 'A good middling one, nine.' She pulled a spare set from the bag at her feet.

The pair I'd brought were too big.

'You'd need very thick wool for those,' she said.

She showed me how to cast on. She was very quick, and at first I was clumsy, but I soon had thirty stitches in the red wool I'd brought. She showed how to do the basic stitch, 'garter stitch', she called it — needle through the stitch, pull the wool around, draw it through and onto the next one. We did thirty stitches and thirty rows, and then we cast off. Each square was an achievement.

'What are we going to do with them, Mum?'

'We'll sew them together to make a rug.'

'We'll need hundreds.'

'Yes, but we have time.'

The nurses brought her wool, half-used balls all in different colours and textures, some fluffy mohair, others she called crepe, and even thick wool, like heavy jumpers. Some squares had three or more colours. We used any little remnant we had.

Sometimes Mum did a fancy stitch, twisting the needles around to make a pattern, but for the time being I stuck with a plain stitch.

'Soon,' she said, 'I'll show you a purl.'

We didn't talk much, just knitted — square after square after square. They piled up around us, and I thought of the rug they would become.

CHAPTER 53

COLIN BRENNAN

FRIDAY, 17 JUNE

I WAS AT ANOTHER MEETING WITH SARAH SOLIMAN IN THE stuffy visitor's parlour.

'Bernadette's made very good progress, and we need to plan for her transition from in-patient to out-patient,' she said. She wanted to continue to see Bernadette weekly, but claimed that it was time she began a 'structured' return to daily life.

Dr Soliman loved her jargon.

'What do you mean by structured?' I asked.

'Weekend visits home for a time, then full-time supported living with her family, and finally moving to independent living, if that's what is necessary.'

I wasn't surprised. Hospital beds were scarce even in private institutions. But I was alarmed. There was nowhere for Bernadette to go. Her home was a pile of rubble, even now being cleared so the land could be sold. Leo's house was out of the question, and although I had an appointment with an agent to inspect a three-bedroom unit on St. Kilda Road that afternoon, I had nowhere to offer her yet. I was also sceptical about Sarah Soliman's assessment of Bernadette's progress. According to Leo, who visited her weekly, she was still evasive and withdrawn.

'How do we tell her that her partner's in jail, and that he burned their house to the ground? That she has nowhere to go?' I asked.

'She has to be told, and arrangements will have to be made for her,' the doctor responded. 'Very soon there will be no reason to have her here as an in-patient. It is imperative that she be helped to return to life in the community.'

I almost smiled at the sheer unrealism of that particular goal. Bernadette was terrified of the community.

Dr Soliman thought for a while, and then continued, 'We could organise a bed in a nursing home for a month or so, but I don't advise it. It would mean disrupting her twice, and as you know, Bernadette doesn't cope well with change. She needs to go home.'

'And where precisely *is* home for Bernadette, Dr Soliman?' I asked. The woman was infuriating.

'That's for you and your family to decide, Colin,' she said, standing and gathering her notes.

Once again I was dismissed.

I dreaded living with Bernadette. The mess, the lack of initiative, the inability to care for herself, but I would never, ever, leave it to Alison again.

No, Bernadette will have to live with us.

CHAPTER 54
LEO BRENNAN
FRIDAY, 17 JUNE

It fell to me to tell Bernie about Harry.

'Thanks Dad,' I said sarcastically when he asked me to do it, but I knew it had to be me. So the doctor sat in Bernie's room with us while I outlined every detail: Harry's crime; his confession to manslaughter; his torching of the house on the morning he was arrested; and his eighteen-year sentence.

She was as impassive as ever. Did she already know some of it? Perhaps she no longer cared what happened to her. She only asked one question. 'Where am I going to live?'

'With Dad and Alison. Dad's buying a place here in Melbourne.'

That was new territory for me. I had no idea what was in Bernie's mind. She showed no grief for Harry and expressed no desire to communicate with him. There was only, what seemed at the time, a resigned acceptance of the arrangements.

'Would you like to ask me anything, Bernie?'

'No, everyone's been very kind,' she said.

Later, when I remembered those words, I realised they were a stock phrase. Mum had taught her to be polite.

Then she looked across at the doctor. 'Well, I suppose that's all,' she said.

She wanted me to leave, and I was glad to get back to my car and the agenda of the afternoon. Clients to see, accounts to be sent, and maybe I could carve out some creative time during the coming weekend.

Now I tortured myself about that relieved exit. I too had stared into the dark abyss, and through some force not my own, I had resisted its seduction. I should have stayed longer, insisted that she talk to me, prised open her feelings, made her angry, anything to prevent what she did …

CHAPTER 55
BERNADETTE BRENNAN
FRIDAY, 17 JUNE

They think I'm weak in the head.

Leo told me about Harry, as if I was a half-wit. See, they thought we didn't talk, but we did. We only had each other. And Alison too, but we knew we'd lose her, especially when she left us and went to Daddy's house for the holidays. Yes, I knew then. As soon as she could, she'd be gone, and why not? It wasn't much of a place for a girl to live.

I never met Harry's father, but I knew about him living in the park. Harry told me. And I knew he went there sometimes.

That Sunday he left in the middle of the day, he was tired of me. I wouldn't get out of bed. He was sick of the house, and Alison was away. We had a fight. He called me a dirty, fat, lazy slob, and left.

'Where are you going?' I called after him.

'To get some air.'

He didn't come back, and then Alison came home, and when I told her there was no water, she wanted to get a plumber, and I screamed at her, and then she called Leo and I screamed at him too. Then those people came, and I struggled, but they stuck a needle in me, and that's when I ended up in here.

Just once I saw a newsbreak about the murder of the homeless man at Enterprise Park. I was groggy from the sedatives and the pills they had me on, but even so I knew it was Harry who'd done it. I'd seen that white-hot rage plenty of times, and he was in a black mood when he had left home that day. It would have only taken one flare-up, and the old man wouldn't have stood a chance.

But burning the house! I didn't know about that. All Mummy's things gone! There was nowhere for me to go. Now *I* was the one who was homeless.

Well, it made it easier, really.

Leo was all concerned and considerate with his story, but I didn't trust them — once, maybe Allie, but not now. There was a time when I told myself that she and I would always be together, that she'd take care of me and I of her. We'd live together, just the two of us. I knew now that that would never happen. She was strong-willed, and I could see that she was determined not to be like me.

She'll make her own way.

I knew when she went to Daddy's place without asking me that I'd already lost her.

Sarah had left me alone. I told her I wanted to sleep. They thought I was getting better, so the nurses weren't spying on me so much. I gave them a few smiles … and the knitting.

They think it's good for me. They like it when Alison comes. Soon enough, they think, they'll be packing me off and there'll be someone else in this room.

I had been thinking about this for months, maybe years. I stopped wanting to live a long time ago.

I've left a letter and the knitting for Alison. But now it's time. I won't live with Daddy, him hovering over me, being oh so kind, and pushing me to be someone else. His impatience. Allie's made her choice, and I won't be a burden. I've longed just to disappear. I've daydreamed, fantasised about it. Just nothingness. Darkness and rest.

It was quiet now. The nurses wouldn't come for an hour or so, and I should be able to sneak past the front desk.

I'll wait till there are a few visitors in the lobby and slip out through them. I would have done it with pills, but they watch you like a hawk until you swallow them. No, this is better. Just a block to walk and then onto the highway. I won't step onto the tracks until the very last second. It will be quick.

CHAPTER 56

COLIN BRENNAN

FRIDAY, 17 JUNE

I WAS SITTING IN MY CAR WAITING FOR THE ESTATE AGENT TO arrive when the newsflash came over the radio. At the time it just seemed like a strange coincidence that I had been on that highway in Box Hill that morning, consulting with Bernadette's doctor. Leo had called me and reported that his sister had reacted calmly to the news about Harry, and that she was now resting. She had agreed that it was best that she live with Alison and me.

'We can make this work, Dad.'

Those were Leo's words. There was no reason for concern, so I met with the agent, inspected the property and made an appointment to bring Alison to see it at the weekend.

Now every word of that newsflash rang in my head.

A middle-aged woman has been hit by a tram on the Maroondah Highway in Box Hill. Paramedics arrived on the scene in minutes, but the woman could not be revived. It is believed that she was a patient at a nearby psychiatric hospital. The tram driver is being treated for shock and trauma. 'She just stepped in front of the tram. There was nothing I could do to avoid her,' he told police. Passengers on the crowed tram have been offered counselling. More details in our afternoon bulletin.

CHAPTER 57
ALISON BRENNAN
FOUR MONTHS LATER

Monday, 3 October

I'M ALWAYS DREAMING ABOUT HOUSES.

Last night it was a big, empty double-storey house. I was dancing in the space, twirling and jumping to some music in my head. Then lots of people came with boxes of stuff, and furniture, and clothes and bedding. I had to unpack and sort it. The people just sat around, doing nothing. They were talking and laughing about me. As soon as I had one box unpacked and everything put away, there was another and another, until I knew I would never finish. I just sat there in all the clutter. I couldn't get through it.

I woke from those dreams with my heart beating fast, and it always took a few minutes for me to remember where I was.

There was another dream. One day in the newspaper, I read about a little removable house they called the Shacky. It was like a doll's house, just big enough for one person. You could move it anywhere. In my dream, I moved it to a high cliff overlooking the ocean, and I lived there all alone with the wind blowing through it.

Grandpa and I now lived in this apartment on the seventeenth floor of a block on St Kilda Road. It was just a short tram ride to school. I liked it right away because it was empty — empty and clean. The kitchen was all stainless steel and I had my own bathroom. The big windows in the living area showed a view of Albert Park Lake and the golf course, and beyond that a glimpse of the bay. There was not much furniture, just what we needed. Grandpa brought some things from Golden Beach, and Leo and Trent stocked the kitchen as a housewarming gift.

There was a spare bedroom, the one Mum would have had. But I couldn't go in there. Not yet.

I loved cooking in the kitchen, but I cleaned it obsessively.

'That's enough, Alison,' Grandpa always said.

But I had to do it. Maybe it was a way of filling the emptiness that was there instead of Mum. Mrs Goodall said that she understood why I felt guilty. She said that family members usually did feel like that after a suicide, but that it was not my fault. 'Your mother made her own decision,' she said. 'Nothing you did would have stopped her.'

In my room I had my bed, Grandma's desk and a bookcase. There was a huge built-in wardrobe where everything else was stored. Leo called it 'spartan,' and then gave me his latest little gift. Today it was an oil burner with some sandalwood oil, because he knew I liked the smell. It was burning gently in my room now.

Schoolwork was the easiest part of my life. When I was studying, I could forget everything for a time. I loved the feeling I got when I worked through a task and it was finished and I knew it was good. That was why I hadn't given up on my schoolwork. It let me be somewhere else.

When I was studying, I didn't hear in my mind the sounds of the tram thwacking into her soft body. I didn't see her blood and broken bones, her dead face. If I didn't find distractions, the hollowness and emptiness inside overtook me. So I studied. I moved from one thing to the next, never stopping for long.

EVERYONE in my Year knew that my mother had died. The Co-ordinator must have told them on one of the days I was away. They were kind. There were hugs and offers of support. Kids who'd never spoken to me before gave me little gifts, a chocolate, a card or a flower. Rosa never left me. In all the classes we took together, she saved a seat for me.

Every day for the first week she brought me something delicious for lunch — rice paper rolls or a slice of quiche. 'Dad sent it for you,' she'd say. She gave me her notes from the classes I'd missed and came to the apartment so we could do homework together. She didn't want anything from me. She didn't ask for details of Mum's death and I didn't tell her. I'm learning from Rosa how to be a friend.

ONE DAY in my first week back, Mr Jordan asked me to stay for a moment after class. I hoped he didn't want to talk about Mum. I was shy, and sometimes I found people's sympathy embarrassing.

But he just said, 'I'm so sorry about your mother, Alison.'

Don't cry, don't cry, I warned myself.

'I know you like poetry. I have something for you.' He went to his desk and brought me a book of poems called *Border of a Dream*, by Antonio Machado. 'He's a Spanish poet who wrote during the 1920s and 30s,' Mr Jordan explained. 'I love his work. There's one I've marked for you.'

I turned to the page to where he'd inserted a bookmark, and I began to read the poem. Mr Jordan had underlined some passages.

Traveller, the road is only
your footprint, and no more;
traveller, there's no road,
the road is your travelling.

Going becomes the road
and if you look back
you will see a path
none can tread again.

When the goldfinch can't sing,
when the poet's a wanderer,
when nothing aids our prayer.
'Traveller there's no road
the road is your travelling…'

Step by step, line by line.

'At times in my life when I don't know what direction to take, I read that poem,' he said. 'It gives me courage and insight to keep going. We make our own path, one step at a time. As the poet says, "there's no road; the road is your travelling."'

How kind he was. I was a real person to him, not just one of the hundreds of students he taught every week. I didn't know what to say. 'Thank you, I'll bring it back in a week or so.'

'No, Alison, it's yours. Keep it. I can get another copy.'

'But it has your notes in it.'

'And now you can add your own notes.'

THAT NIGHT I sat on my bed and read Machado's poem aloud over and over again.

Yes, I thought, *I can make my path by walking. One step after another. And one day I will have learnt not to look back to the path that no one can tread again.*

Grandpa and I were walking, step-by-step, making new, happier, paths.

We were hesitant, and then Nadia came.

CHAPTER 58

COLIN BRENNAN

SATURDAY, 8 OCTOBER

FOR THE FIRST TWO MONTHS, ALISON AND I WERE LIKE TWO shipwrecked sailors, bobbing on the ocean in an untrustworthy lifeboat, unable to control our direction. We passed each other in the big, sparsely furnished apartment like stunned survivors of a disaster.

Then Nadia came, bringing a bright rush of colour into our beige dwelling.

'What a wonderful view,' she exclaimed, sweeping across to the big windows. 'I can see right to the bay.'

Then she commented, 'But Colin, it's empty. Where is your furniture?'

'Oh, you know. We're making do.'

'Making do? You're camping! Where do you eat?'

I pointed to the two armchairs that I'd brought from the house at Golden Beach. They were positioned in front of the window, and they were the only furniture in the large living area. 'We're living rather casually.'

Nadia was horrified. 'You're eating on your laps? Oh dear. And only two armchairs. Where is a visitor to sit?'

I was a little embarrassed. In the weeks after Bernadette's funeral, I had focused all my attention on Alison. Understanding her horror at the conditions in which she had lived with her parents, I had decided not to overwhelm her with possessions that I alone may consider necessary.

Nadia would have none of it.

'But Colin, this is not civilised. We must go shopping. Show me the rest of the apartment.'

She gasped at the space in my bedroom with its single fold out bed and small table on which my neglected memoirs sat. She tut-tutted over Alison's room with its one bed against the window, Mary's desk the only other furniture.

'Where are her friends to sleep when they come to stay?' she asked.

When she walked into the empty spare bedroom and gazed about her, I realised that in my reluctance to clutter the place, I had sacrificed convenience and homeliness.

'You must make this into a study, Colin,' she said, 'where Alison can read and work, and you can write.'

Alison returned from the market then, with bags of fruit and vegetables, which she put on the kitchen bench. She was startled for a moment, and then she held out her hand to Nadia.

'Professor Godlewski, it's good to see you again.'

Nadia scooped her up in a hug. 'I'm Nadia and I'm longing to talk with you. But first we must take your Grandpa shopping. Colin, dear heart, make me a coffee and then we will devise a plan of attack.'

That I could do. Leo and Trent had given us their coffee machine when they upgraded to a newer model.

As I made the coffee, Nadia and Alison put the food away. Alison was shy, but she didn't appear to be overwhelmed by Nadia, as I feared she might have been. They chatted about the apartment, Nadia exclaiming over its space and convenience.

'We'll begin with the Sacred Heart Mission Op Shop,' she declared.

Op Shop? I had never been in an Op Shop in my life.

'Aren't they… aren't they … you know, for poor people?' I asked, handing Nadia her coffee.

Alison giggled.

'Oh, Colin.' Nadia laughed. 'You *are* behind the times. Everyone shops at Op Shops. You can get the most marvellous second-hand furniture.'

'But … is it … clean?' This was a new world for me.

More laughter. Too late, I realised what a stuffy old thing I sounded like.

THAT WAS the beginning of a day trawling the second-hand shops around St Kilda and Fitzroy. By evening we had a rather lovely lounge suite in an ivory-coloured brocade, which we positioned in front of the window; a glass-topped dining table with six straight-backed chairs, their seats covered in a similar coloured fabric; a bright circular floor rug with splotches of blue, red, green and gold to offset the grey of the carpet; another single bed and a big, art deco style dresser for Alison's room; a double bed and new mattress for my room; a large glass and wood computer desk and ergonomic chair for the spare bedroom, and a further bookcase to take the overflow of Alison's study materials. One of the Golden Beach armchairs was relegated to the spare room, and the other to my bedroom.

'You can read the paper here in the sun,' Nadia declared.

All of the furniture was purchased for astonishingly low prices from clean, orderly shops much of whose wares, the assistants told me, were donated from deceased estates.

'Good that you're giving it a new home,' one of these assistants commented, as we arranged delivery of the lounge suite.

. . .

THAT EVENING, we sat over dinner at our new dining suite and watched the sun set in Melbourne's west. Later, Nadia and Alison pored together over Stasiewicz's book of poems. Nadia's dark head was close to Alison's as she tentatively translated.

'Polish is my first language,' I heard her say. 'It was the language my parents taught me. But because I use English every day, it's quite hard for me to translate these poems. In translation, the intention of the poet, what he really wanted to say, may be lost.'

'But you have to try, don't you?' Alison asked.

'Yes, and I know enough about your grandfather, about his history, the things he cared about, his beliefs and values, to do it as well as possible.'

I watched her, the care with which she handled the dilapidated little book.

Suddenly I had a clear, vivid but utterly terrifying revelation.

I love this woman.

CHAPTER 59

ALISON BRENNAN

SATURDAY, 15 OCTOBER

LAST TUESDAY WE WERE AT THE LOCKERS AS USUAL, GETTING organised for the day, when Selma Ferguson came up to Rosa with a beaming smile.

'Hey, Rosa,' she said, as if they were best friends.

'Hey, Selma,' Rosa said, continuing to stack books in her bag.

'Do you want to hang out with us at after school? We're going into the city.'

'No thanks, Alison and I have stuff to do.' Rosa gave me a sideways glance, her eyebrows raised, questioning.

What does she want?

Selma stared at me. She clearly hadn't factored me in.

'Okay. Another time then.' She turned to go away, and then turned back.

'I met your brother on Saturday.'

'Gio? He's a little young for you isn't he, Selma?'

'No, Dario.'

Rosa pretended not to be interested. 'Yeah? Where did you meet him?'

'At that music store he works at in Elizabeth Street. He

asked us what school we went to and said that his sister was there too. He told us your name.'

'Oh, that's nice.' Rosa was going to make this hard for Selma.

'He helped me with a song I was looking for, and I wanted to call and thank him. Would you give me his number?'

Rosa stopped packing her bag, and turned towards Selma. 'Look, if you want Dario's phone number you'll have to ask him yourself. I'm not his personal assistant. And besides, I've got a fruit and vegetable stall to attend to.'

An icy, prolonged stare, and then Selma turned and flounced off.

We giggled, high-fived each other, and went into homeroom.

JUST AS ROLL call was beginning, Rosa whispered to me, 'Hey, Allie, you know Sam, that boy that sits at the back of the room with his mate Matt?'

'Yes.'

'Don't look at him, don't turn around,' she hissed.

'Yes, Sam. What about him?'

'He wants me to go out with him on Saturday.'

'Wow. Of course you said yes.' Sam was nice. He was smarter than most of the other boys, and he didn't treat girls as if they were just there for decoration. If we had a mixed gender group assignment, all the girls wanted Sam to be in their group. He pulled his weight.

'I said I'd let him know.'

'You said what? You're crazy. Everyone wants to go out with Sam.'

'Alison and Rosa, please keep the conversation for recess.' That was our homeroom teacher, Mrs Henry.

I brought it up again as we walked to our first class. 'What's the problem, Rosa? Sam's cute … and nice.'

'Yes, I know, but I haven't had much to do with boys. With all the mess in the family in Sydney, I was always babysitting Gio. My weekends got used up.'

'All the more reason for you to say yes to Sam now. Do something good for yourself.' I was starting to talk like Mrs Goodall.

Rosa just shrugged and didn't say anything more about it for the rest of the day.

THAT AFTERNOON after school we were supposedly doing exam revision together. We sat on the floor in the living area of Rosa's house with the TV on softly in the background. Our books and notes were spread around us.

'Sam asked me again, Allie. He wants us to go ice-skating.'

'So go.' I couldn't see why Rosa was reluctant.

'I don't know.' Rosa shrugged her shoulders.

I was astonished. 'Why don't you know? Don't you like ice-skating?'

'I love it.'

'Well?'

'Look, Allie, I don't know Sam very well. What am I going to talk to him about?'

'But you've got lots in common … school, teachers … and he's in the debating team. You could talk about that.'

'That's part of it. He's smart.'

'And so are you.'

Rosa paused. 'Allie, if I asked you a really big favour, would you do it for me?' She took my hand and held it.

'You know I would if I could.'

'Come with me.'

She couldn't be serious. 'Come with you on a date? You're joking!'

'Please.'

'What? I can't come with you when you go out with a boy. It's weird.'

'Well, I won't go. That's it.' Rosa dropped my hand and turned away.

'Rosa, don't be crazy. Anyway, I've never been ice-skating. I'd be hopeless.'

'You'd pick it up easily. You're very sporty.'

'Sam would hate it, Rosa. Your friend coming along to supervise. How creepy.'

We left it then and went back to our biology revision.

FIVE MINUTES LATER, Dario sauntered out from the kitchen eating a hot dog. He'd obviously been listening. 'Going on a date, little Rosa?' he asked.

She raised her eyebrows at me. 'God, you're annoying. Don't you have somewhere to be?'

'Word of advice. If you want Allie to go with you, you really need to have another guy there. That way your guy won't feel outnumbered.'

The idea made sense, but where were we going to get another guy?

'Guys who want to go ice-skating with girls on a Saturday afternoon don't grow on trees, Dario,' Rosa said sarcastically.

'Well, I could come.'

'What, to chaperone me?'

'No … sort of like a date for Allie … a pretend date. Then you have two couples and it looks normal.'

Rosa was quiet for a minute.

Was she actually thinking about the idea?

'Do you mean it, Dario? What about your job?'

'I'm owed a few hours off. I'll do it for you. And it has the advantage that you'll have wheels. We can pick what's his name up on the way.'

Rosa looked at me, pleading.

What was I getting myself into? Ice-skating? I'd never done it before, and with gorgeous Marlon Brando-featured Dario there, I was bound to make a complete fool of myself.

But I owed Rosa. 'Okay … okay.'

'Yes!' Rosa hugged me tight.

'Don't let me make a complete idiot of myself, please,' I said as I hugged her back.

I WAS PETRIFIED. Over the next few days I watched every YouTube video I could find about ice-skating. Choosing the correct size shoe; the starting posture; how to keep your balance; even how to fall and get up again. I practised it all in my room, but I shouldn't have worried. Saturday was the best fun I'd ever had.

First I watched Sam and Rosa skating together. They glided, wheeled and weaved holding hands as if they'd been skating together forever. Then Dario and Rosa together. It was beautiful. They were like graceful birds, circling each other, moving away then coming back together in another dance. They reminded me of a film clip I had seen of a pair of brolgas.

When they came back to where Sam and I were sitting, I said, 'You two look amazing together.'

'Yes, we used to do a lot of ice-skating together as a family in Sydney,' Rosa said.

'Your turn now, Allie,' Dario said.

Suddenly, my heart was in my mouth, and I was awkward and shy, but he patiently took me through the basics, and before long I was able to stay upright and to glide as if I wasn't just a beginner. Dario stayed with me and we circled the outside of the rink until I was ready to be more adventurous.

'You're fit,' Dario said. 'Most people can't do it so easily the first time.'

The afternoon went too quickly. Soon all four of us were skating together holding hands and whooping with excitement.

We had milkshakes and hamburgers at the café, and then Sam and Rosa went for one more skate together. Dario and I talked hesitantly. He told me about his university course in ecological science, but he said that this real interest was music. One day he wanted to own a store that specialised in twentieth-century music.

'Which artists?'

'The King, of course, Elvis Presley, but really all of the artists and bands from the 1960s and 70s. It was an incredible era in music. And I love vinyl records. I have a massive collection. I'm always scouting around garage sales and bargain shops to find more. Well, that's me. Tell me about yourself, Allie.'

'Nothing much to tell. Year Eleven at the same school as Rosa. She's my best friend.'

'Do you like school?'

'Yeah, I do.'

'Rosa says that you're clever, as well as hard working.'

'Yeah, I guess I am.' My tongue seemed to have developed a bad case of warts.

'I hear your mum died. I'm sorry.'

'Thanks. I hope you don't mind Dario, but I'm not ready yet to talk about it.'

'I get that.'

He was nice. He didn't seem to be the know-all bore that Rosa had described him as. He just seemed ordinary, and a bit shy like me. But I didn't get relationships between brothers and sisters, never having had one.

We watched Rosa and Sam for a while, and then Dario turned to me again. 'Can I pay you a compliment?'

I could feel myself blushing.

'You have really beautiful hair.'

Now I was bright red. How embarrassing.

Then Dario said, 'You're different from other girls. You don't flirt.'

I didn't know how to flirt. My life until now hadn't had much room for it. 'Thanks, Dario. You're nice too. Different from what I expected.'

'Different from what Rosa told you? Well, families *can* get on each other's nerves.'

Then Sam and Rosa came back and we were in Dario's car heading home. Sam and Rosa held hands in the back seat while the most soulful, emotional voice I'd ever heard sang through Dario's sound system. He was listening intently with the volume turned up loud.

'Who is it, Dario?'

'Don't you recognise the voice? The King, Elvis, singing "American Trilogy". It always makes me a bit emotional.'

Elvis Presley died before I was born, but right then in Dario's car, it felt like he was singing just for me.

CHAPTER 60

LEO BRENNAN

WEDNESDAY, 19 OCTOBER

The old dog!

Last night, the Judge came to see me.

'Need to talk to you about something,' he had said. 'Just you and me. It's a family matter.'

Okay, so Trent's not family! But I wasn't going to argue the point until I knew what it was about. 'Why so secretive, Dad?'

'Not secretive really. I just wanted to tell you about something and get your advice.'

This was new. Never once had the Judge asked my advice about anything.

'Okay, Dad, let's go outside.'

It was pleasant on our tiny back veranda. I could smell the jasmine that hung over the fence, and hear Chester in the corner gnawing on a resurrected bone.

I brought out a cup of coffee for each of us.

'Okay, fire away.'

'Well, Leo, this will be a surprise, perhaps a shock. I'm … I'm hoping to marry again.'

By some miracle I didn't fall backwards off my chair and

spill my coffee, but I was flabbergasted. 'Married? You've never said anything about this?'

'No, I haven't.'

'Is it someone I know?'

You've met her once. Nadia Godlewski … Professor Nadia Godlewski. She was at Borys Stasiewicz's funeral.'

'That Polish woman who sang?' I recalled that she'd helped Trent and Jossie on the murder case.

'Yes, she's a Professor of Polish literature. She was instrumental in identifying the old man.'

'Does she know about this?' Perhaps, I thought, he was being fanciful, imagining a mutual attraction where none existed.

'Yes, we've been seeing each other regularly for some months.'

At his age! Sneaking around with a new love. 'What about the age difference, Dad?'

'She's sixty-eight and I'm eighty. It's not such a big difference.'

'She didn't look anything like sixty-eight the day I met her.'

'No, she's extremely healthy and full of vitality. She works full time and intends to keep doing so well into the future. She's applying for funding to set up a Centre for Polish Studies at the university.'

'Well, I must say, Dad, you know how to drop a bombshell. But what about Alison, if Nadia accepts you?'

'Alison will stay with me, of course, in the apartment. Eventually she will own it. If Nadia accepts my proposal, she will decide for herself where she lives. She has a house near the university and will probably want to keep it. Those things can be worked out.'

He'd obviously been making plans. 'What do you want from me, Dad?'

'Your reaction? Your advice? Perhaps even your blessing.'

This was a very different Judge from the one who had blustered and complained about his daughter daring to be ill, on that Monday after we had to have her taken to hospital. It was more than the simple fact that he'd mellowed. No, he had changed in fundamental ways.

His authoritative air had gone, and he was just like any of us now, fumbling, a little scared, hopeful, trying to find his way in the years that were left to him, and yes, humble. It was not a word I ever thought I'd use about him, but faced with the miracle of unexpected love, he was humble. The arrogance of all his certainties had left him.

In that moment I felt that our roles were reversed, that he was the nervous son hoping for his father's approval, and I was the one who could put a seal on his happiness or deny it to him.

Suddenly, I was inordinately fond of the old fellow. 'My reaction, Dad? Surprise, even shock, but not sadness. You've been alone for almost twenty years. My reaction is happiness for you. My advice? Do it. Ask her. "Screw your courage to its sticking place." That's Shakespeare, isn't it?'

'Yes, Macbeth.'

'My blessing, Dad? You have it in spades.' I reached across to shake his hand, but then there was another surprise in that night of surprises …

He stood and pulled me into an embrace. 'Thank you, Son, thank you.'

We both had tears in our eyes. But there was one more thing. 'You know that I'll tell Trent. We tell each other everything.'

He just nodded. I didn't think he cared.

CHAPTER 61

JOSSIE WALLACHIA

FRIDAY, 21 OCTOBER

THE SPRING WEATHER WAS STARTING TO PENETRATE THE CITY, and I was in Bourke Street Mall trying to while away a week of leave. I didn't do leisure well. I was standing in the middle of a three-deep crowd, listening to a busker — all electronic canned music and a lot of Bob Dylan — when I saw her.

The long, golden hair had recently had the attention of a skilled colourist and stylist. The perfect makeup accentuated her high cheekbones, dramatic eyes and wide, generous mouth. She wore a classic, tailored, black pantsuit that, even if I had been inclined to buy it, would have cost me two months' salary. It was offset by a creamy, ivory silk blouse and the highest of black heels. Her jewellery was understated-tiny diamond ear studs and a pendant with a single ruby. Her beauty was magnetic, more so that not long ago I had seen her in a sharply different context. I had to talk to her.

Moving to her side, I touched her arm lightly, distracting her from the singer. 'Bett.'

She turned to me questioning, then her face lit up in recognition.

'Little Miss Detective.' Then to my surprise she kissed me. She smelled expensive. 'Is it really you? How good to see you.'

The same cultured, educated voice, still husky from a lifetime of smoking, although the long fingers that rested on my arm were no longer stained with nicotine, and the manicure was recent. 'Can we get a coffee? My treat this time.' She took my arm.

We found a teashop and Bett went through the ritual of ordering her Earl Grey tea while I settled for a cappuccino.

'You look wonderful, Bett. What's going on in your life? Where are you living?'

'With my mother in the family home in Caulfield. Yes, I know you're shocked, especially after the way I spoke about my parents and relatives and their religious ways. But this is what happened. Do you remember Hobie's funeral and the Polish woman who sang that Catholic prayer over his coffin? '

'Yes, Professor Nadia Godlewski. I remember it well.'

'Well, it started something for me. Something about traditions. Seeing Hobie buried alone in a country he never really adopted, so far from the homeland that he'd fought for and written about, that he loved. And no one to bury him except strangers, with only one person to pray for him in his own language. It felt terribly lonely. I loved him, you know, Jossie.'

'Yes, Bett, I know.'

'Then to find out that it was his own son who killed him. What a terrible thing. Without Hobie around to talk to, sleeping in that park began to feel desperate. I was desolate without him.'

'Dangerous too.'

'Yes, when I look back I see that it was very dangerous, but as you know I wouldn't admit it. Then the Rabbi from our synagogue tracked me down — don't ask me how — he came to the park and found me. I was ashamed, so conscious of how I looked, dirty and sleeping rough. He told me that my father was dying.' Bett paused for a moment to sip her tea. 'I was just in time. I turned up on their doorstep two hours before he died. Mother didn't comment, just brought me in. "You'd better have a bath, Elizabeth," was all she said.'

Bett smiled wryly at the memory. 'Seeing my father dying and remembering Hobie made me want to turn back to my religion. It was quite sudden and unexpected. I didn't want Papa to die without the dignity he deserved. I wanted him to have all the respect that came from our history. So we did everything to the letter. He was a good Jew, one of the last of the *Dunera* boys, but a great Australian too, a philanthropist. Mother and I anointed and dressed the body, lit the candles and recited the blessing. He was buried the next day with all the correct observances, and after that the family sat Shiva for him for seven days. There are all kinds of regulations around Shiva, and we fulfilled every one of them. I was proud of that. I felt that we'd given him proper honour.'

This was a different Bett, claiming her Jewishness, no longer in retreat from it and resenting its hold on her.

'Now I'm in the twelve month period of mourning for a parent, so there are restrictions around what I can do. I'm the only child, so although it's supposed to be a son who recites Kiddush for a parent, I'm doing it for my father every day until the mourning period is over.'

How interesting life is, I thought.

The simple, spontaneous act of Nadia Godlewski singing a traditional prayer for Hobie had opened up in Bett a stream of memory that brought her back to her family and religion.

'Are you going to keep living with your mother?'

'Oh yes. She's well enough but frail. I couldn't leave her alone. When she goes, I'll observe all the rituals for her just as she'd expect. We're getting on well, though. We need each other.'

I was genuinely glad for her, glad that she was safe and happy. 'I'm so pleased we ran into each other, Bett. I've often thought of you and hoped you were okay.'

'Yes, I'm more than okay. I'm happy. Jossie, I was

wondering about Hobie's granddaughter, that lovely girl. Would you bring her to see me, just once? It would be a last chance to talk about Hobie.' She scribbled an address and phone number on the page of a small notebook, tore it out and pushed it toward me.

'Alison's had a frightful year, Bett. As you know her father's in jail for Hobie's killing, and her mother recently died. She has exams and holidays coming up. Is it okay if I talk to her about this next year, when her life is more settled?'

'Of course. I'll be there waiting.' Then she stood and embraced me.

I watched her elegant figure weaving though the city crowds until it was swallowed up.

Sometimes in this job, things go right almost by accident.

CHAPTER 62

TRENT GRIERSON

SATURDAY, 22 OCTOBER

GOING THROUGH THE ROUTINE AGAIN, THE SCANNER, THE PAT down, the dogs, showing my ID, getting checked off the approved list, and then going through to the big, cold visitors' area with its hard plastic tables and chairs, everything immovable. Waiting for Harry to come through the door. I did this once a month.

I was the one who had been deputised to tell him about Bernie's suicide a few days after it happened. I couldn't read his face as we spoke. He asked a few questions.

'Did she die right away?'

'Yes, the paramedics said it would have been instant.' I had rehearsed some simple straightforward answers.

He breathed deeply — a sign of relief, perhaps. 'Did she leave anything?'

'Only a letter for Alison.' I wished I could have told him that she'd left a message for him, but I couldn't lie.

'Where's she buried?'

'In the family plot next to her mother.' Short, sharp, straight to the point.

And then that was it. He said nothing more.

'I'm sorry, Harry,' I said.

'Yeah, well, it was probably always going to happen; she was a sick girl.'

On this visit, nothing much had changed. His big frame shuffled through the door, and he came towards me, not exactly smiling, but pleased to see me, I thought.

'G'day mate,' he said as he shook my hand.

I no longer felt that fury towards him that I felt that Sunday when he helped me clear out the junk in his front yard. I would never understand what made him attack old Hobie, and maybe he didn't understand himself, but all I felt for him now was pity.

Our regular visits were mostly silent, but I would keep going. It was another link between him and Alison. We exchanged information.

He seemed to be fine in jail, and was actually the 'go to' guy for anything mechanical around the prison. Not surprising, Leo said he could fix anything, although why he didn't apply his skills in his own home was beyond me. He had even learnt to read and write in afternoon classes.

'Basic literacy, they call it,' he said. 'One day soon I'll be able to write Allie a letter.' He grinned at that.

We talked about Allie. He longed for news of her, even though he talked to her on the phone every week. I told him what was on the news, and he passed on bits of prison gossip. He looked well. Today he told me that he worked out in the gym most days.

'The food's okay,' he said.

Our silences weren't uncomfortable. He was a silent man, but I sensed he was not unhappy.

'Allie wants to come with me next time,' I told him.

'No! Not here. It's too rough. One day they'll send me to minimum security. She can come then.'

At the end, he shook my hand again. 'Good to see you, mate. Thanks for coming.'

The security routine again, then out into the air, and through the Melbourne traffic home.

There were worse blokes than Harry. He was a victim of humanity's thirst for war, just as his father and millions of others were. But Alison … she, I was sure, would rise above the bloodlust and cruelty that had stained her family. She would survive her history.

CHAPTER 63
ALISON BRENNAN
WEDNESDAY, 7 DECEMBER

LAST NIGHT WAS OUR SCHOOL'S PRESENTATION AND SPEECH night.

We all had to be there in uniform to listen to the Principal report on the year, and to reward student achievements. The Year Eleven teachers lined up with the prizes for the best student in each subject. I watched Mr Jordan come to the microphone.

'The Year Eleven prize for excellence in the study of literature goes to Alison Brennan.'

I felt a jolt of shock in my chest and became aware that Rosa, sitting next to me, was whispering, 'Go,.. go.'

Trembling slightly, I walked up the steps onto the stage to shake Mr Jordan's hand.

'Really wonderful work all year, Alison,' he said.

I looked out to the audience and saw Grandpa with Nadia, Leo and Trent. My family was applauding — they looked so proud of me. Then in the shadows at the back of the hall, I thought I saw two beloved figures standing near the exit — one tall, the other short and round.

Mum and Dad.

But no, it was just a flicker of light. For a moment I felt as if I was out of my body, as if this was happening to another girl, and then I just felt glad that the horrible year was ending, and that somehow I had come through it.

My prize was a big, heavy book, *An Anthology of Australian Poetry since 1788.*

This is for you, Mum and Dad, I told them silently, as I left the stage.

CHAPTER 64
ALISON BRENNAN
FRIDAY, 9 DECEMBER

TODAY, SCHOOL FINISHED FOR THE YEAR.

I took flowers to Mrs Goodall, to thank her for the hours I'd spent in her office talking about my life. She gave me a card with a photo of a deep blue ocean and a single seagull flying above the waves. Inside she'd written, *Fly in freedom into the wind, Alison. Your friend, Stella Goodall.*

Tomorrow, Grandpa and Nadia were going to be married at the Catholic Church in Richmond, where there was a Polish chaplain, a friend of Nadia's. I had a new dress and shoes, and Nadia said I should have a hat. So we went shopping together and I bought a straw hat with a small brim in the same blue as my dress. Nadia called it a 'fedora'.

'It looks lovely on you, Alison,' Grandpa said, but after tomorrow I probably wouldn't wear it again. I didn't like hats.

Grandpa asked me how I felt about him marrying Nadia. I meant it when I said I thought it was a brilliant idea. I could see that they were in love. When she was there, he followed her around with his eyes, and they were always giving each other secret little smiles. I liked Nadia a lot, but I was pleased when she said that she didn't want to be a grandmother to me.

'We'll be friends,' she said. 'I don't want to be anyone's

grandmother.'

That's good, I thought.

This year, I've learnt more about my mum's mother than I ever knew before, and I found out that I had a Polish grandfather who was a poet during the war. Then Dad went to jail and Mum died. I didn't want any more changes on the 'relations front'.

On Boxing Day, Grandpa, Nadia and I were leaving for Poland for a three-week visit.

'Not work this time, Colin, I promise,' Nadia said. 'I'll show you my beautiful country, and I want you to meet my relatives.'

We were going to have an overnight stop in London on the way, and on the way back, spend a week in Paris.

'I want you to see everything, Alison,' Nadia said. 'We'll begin in Krakow — so many art galleries and museums, so much history. Then I want to take you to Warsaw, where your grandfather lived and fought, and where he wrote his poetry.'

We were also going to go to the Baltic Sea, although Nadia said it was going to be freezing, and we were going to see the palaces and grand buildings that had been restored.

And Auschwitz.

'Horrendous as it is, it is important to know what was done to your grandfather's people and millions of Jews. We'll pay our respects to the dead there, and pray that nothing like that ever happens again.'

I was so excited. It was to be my first time on a plane; my first time out of Victoria, and my first overseas trip.

Before school started again, there would be time for a week at Golden Beach, for Grandpa and Nadia, me and Rosa.

ON THE SIDE of my desk there's a small cabinet with a fancy latch. I bought a padlock and key for it because I put all the things that were mine alone there. There were two beautiful shells that I found on the sand at Golden Beach; there was my grandfather's book of poems; and there was the note Dario sent me through Rosa after we went ice-skating.

Hi Allie, I had a great time on Saturday. I hope you'll go out with me again sometime. Dario.

I asked Rosa to thank him for the note, but I didn't write back. I put it in my desk and I would think about it next year.

And now there was the seagull card I got from Mrs Goodall — and this:

Dear Alison,

It has to be this way. I can't go on anymore, and I don't want to. I was never strong enough for this world, so I tried to hide from it. But you are strong and brave like my dear mother. I want you to do everything I was too afraid to do. Please don't forget me. I loved you, but I couldn't give you a good life. Finish the rug we were making together. Maybe you'll show it to your children when you tell them about me.

Darling, I hope when you do that, your words are kind.

Your loving mum.

I had unfolded and folded the note so many times that it had started to crack along the seams. I did finish the rug — two hundred squares. Nadia, Rosa and I stitched it together bit by bit, and now it lies across my bed, warm and colourful.

Maybe one day I will have children and I can show it to them, telling them about their grandmother, who, for all her pain, loved me the best she could.

Yes, Mum, my words will be kind.

I won't forget Mum, or Dad either. When he comes out of jail, wherever I am, there'll be a place for him.

CHAPTER 65

ALISON BRENNAN

TUESDAY, 20 DECEMBER

IT WAS THE WEEK BEFORE CHRISTMAS, AND TODAY WAS MY seventeenth birthday. Rosa was coming later, and we were going Christmas shopping. Nadia was making a birthday cake and Rosa was going to stay the night.

Tonight I was going to tell her everything — the whole story. She deserved my trust, and I knew now that she wouldn't judge me.

It was early. I was making a cup of coffee when Grandpa came into the kitchen.

'Ah, you're awake. Happy birthday, darling,' he said, kissing me. 'Wait here. I have a gift for you.'

He returned to the bedroom and came back with a small parcel, which he put on the table in front of me. He seemed nervous, excited and a bit jumpy. 'I didn't think anything could have survived that fire,' he said. 'The place was just ash, everything gone. But the contractors I hired to clean out the rubble found it, and they were honest enough to give it to me. It was in an iron box, that's what protected it. It was probably lost for years in that house. I've had it cleaned and re-strung. Open it, dear.'

I tore away the paper and opened the box. Inside was a soft, black velvet bag. I opened the bag and drew them out gently — big, lustrous, gleaming pearls, with a hint of the pink Broome sunset glowing on each round surface.

REFERENCES

1. A Mathews, M Gelder, D Johnston, Agorophobia: Nature and Treatment, Tavistock Publications, London and New York, 1981.
2. J Oppenheimer, Private Demons: The Life of Shirley Jackson, Fawcett Columbine, New York, 1988.
3. R Lukas, The Forgotten Holocaust: The Poles under German Occupation, 1939-1944. Third Edition, Hippocrene Books, New York.

Dear reader,

We hope you enjoyed reading *The Blooming of Alison Brennan*. Please take a moment to leave a review, even if it's a short one. Your opinion is important to us.

Discover more books by Kath Engebretson at https://www.nextchapter.pub/authors/kath-engebretson

Want to know when one of our books is free or discounted? Join the newsletter at http://eepurl.com/bqqB3H

Best regards,
Kath Engebretson and the Next Chapter Team

ABOUT THE AUTHOR

Dr Kathleen Engebretson is a teacher and academic. She wrote her first novel, *Red Dirt Odyssey*, while living in a caravan in the Kimberley town of Kununurra. *The Blooming of Alison Brennan* draws on some of her experiences as a secondary school teacher. Details of her fiction and academic publishing can be found at http://www.kathengebretson.com/

Printed in Great Britain
by Amazon

32080301R00148